Copyright © 2023, Helen Anderson

All rights reserved. No part of this book may be reproduced or distributed in any form without prior written permission from the author, with the exception of non-commercial uses permitted by copyright law.

The Little Book of Everyday People
Helen Anderson

Dedicated to Charlie & Juniper
Who brought the rainbow after the storm.

Acknowledgements

The genesis of this story took root in my mind and numerous notebooks over the span of a decade. Despite my attempts to capture it on paper, the narrative eluded me until an unexpected burst of inspiration struck during one of my daughter's nap traps. Whether fueled by the fog of sleep deprivation or the copious caffeine intake, the words flowed effortlessly, and I found myself unable to resist the urge to write.

To my unwavering supporter, my husband, Charlie – your consistent encouragement has been my steadfast anchor. Thank you for not only being my greatest cheerleader but also for graciously carving out the time for me to mould worlds for others to explore. My journey to this point would not have been possible without you, my love.

A heartfelt appreciation goes to my daughter, Juniper, whose presence provided the essential space and time for me to take this significant step in my writing journey. Your name, meaning healing, took on a profound significance after the loss of your sibling, and I am grateful for the joy you bring to the world.

To my parents, Carol and Peter, who chose the idyllic village that became the backdrop of our family's growth – thank you. Alongside my brother and sister, Tom and Laura, we were enveloped in a community that, to this day, exemplifies genuine care and mutual support. The values instilled during my childhood laid the foundation for love, care, and dedication in my adult life. Thank you.

Finally, my gratitude extends to you, the reader. Thank you for choosing to embark on the journey into the realm of Puckleworth by purchasing my book. I hope it serves as a source of healing, escapism, humour, and nostalgia.

Helen

Chapter One

Nestled among trees on rolling hills of the town of Puckleworth, is the elegant Blossom Cottage. It boasts dollhouse features, which coexist with a grand, century-old oak tree at the edge of its untamed garden. A weathered fence encircles the property, distinguishing it from the others on Willow Lane. Its muted colours contrast with the robins that sit on it.

The fresh green treats in the fields are a magnet for the rabbits, who dart back and forth along the property's hidden boundaries.

Meanwhile, as the blossom buds push through a sheer veil of frost, the sun creeps over the landscape. Its warmth brings soothing hues of rosy skies and vanilla clouds, enveloping the home that stands before us.

Abruptly, a chorus of bird-song penetrates the silence and saturates the modest upstairs bedroom. This melody pulls Ru from one world into the next, and thus awakens her from a heavy sleep.

Upon awakening, she rolls onto her back and winces as she repositions herself on the well-worn mattress. Gently, as she rubs her eyes, she stretches and lets out a long yawn, which is followed by a deep sigh. For a few moments, Ru lies there, paralysed in thought, staring up at the cobwebs that link the beams together.

She shifted her legs to the side, and she braced herself as her feet contacted the dark oak floorboards. To her left, there's an oversized dressing table, missing a mirror; positioned beneath the window. Without hesitation, she threw open the curtains, unveiling the view of the boundless fields that stretched out before her. The beauty took her breath away as she eased back onto the stool to take it all in.

After a few moments Ru notices the chilly confines of the cottage and a bitterness nipped at her toes, prompting her to search for her bed socks. To her surprise, her face brightened with a smile upon discovering a dainty pair of pale pink fuzzy socks that she knew weren't hers. Still, she placed them at the bed's foot and resumed her search for her own. With a wince, she bent down to retrieve them, severely noticing the discomfort in her body, a clear sign of the stress the old mattress had imposed on her.

Ru threw on her cardigan and set off downstairs in search of caffeine. Upon entering the kitchen, she surveyed the room where a wooden table proudly dominated the space. Interestingly, each chair possessed its own unique charm — one with a crucifix and a bible holder on its back, another carved with roses. The third boasted generous armrests reminiscent of a royal household, while the last exuded a quaint charm, speaking of rustic simplicity.

Distinctly positioned, two brass candlesticks with burnt ivory candles graced the table. Next to them, four placemats adorned with farm animals lay centred, all underneath an empty fruit bowl. On the opposite side, copper pots and pans hung from the far wall, their surfaces brightly reflecting the sunlight. Above them, a thin shelf played host to herbs and spices settled in their tiny containers. She shifted her gaze along the sidewall. Ru observed a light-stained Welsh dresser, which was handsomely filled with crockery and a captivating assortment of bone china cups and saucers.

After making her way toward the stove top, she cleaned the kettle out and took another glance out the window. Then she turned on the hob and surveyed the kitchen more intently. Carefully, she collected a spaniel bone china mug from the draining board and sifted through the canisters on the countertop. The small pantry in the corner of the room caught her eye, hopefully it would contain coffee.

Ru balanced precariously on a small wooden step and rummaged around the various tins and bottles before smiling as she spotted the instant coffee pot. Soon after, the kettle whistle commanded Ru's attention. She graciously pretended to ice skate across the kitchen floor in her bed socks. Another smile flashed across her face however, she rapidly suppressed the accompanying memory and brewed herself a cup of coffee.

Ru turned on her heel and headed towards the large fridge, which, to her surprise, swung open with ease. Upon inspecting its contents, she realised it was empty and that she'd forgotten the milk, prompting a frustrated huff and a dramatic flinging of her head backwards. On the bright side, at least there was sugar here.

She fought the cutlery drawer to open but it wouldn't budge. As she rolled her eyes, she added it to her list of jobs and then jimmied it open. With a coffee in hand Ru retraced her steps back into the living room she had walked through.

In one corner stood an oversized lamp. She switched it on, casting a warm glow across the dim room. Eager for some relaxation, she sank into the plush armchair and extended the leg rest, aiming for maximum comfort for her weary legs.

To her left, there was a small fireplace with burn marks tarnishing a faded rug. Adjacent, a magazine rack held old issues of TV Weekly Magazine. Meanwhile, on the arm of the sofa, a pair of glasses and a pen lay poised atop a half-completed crossword puzzle.

As time passed, Ru's eyelids grew heavy. Abruptly, the coo-coo of the clock startled her, causing cool coffee to spill onto her pyjamas. She realised she must have nodded off, so she rubbed her eyes and found her gaze drawn to a turntable. Beside it, a dozen vinyl records lay against each other in a basket.

Curiously, she played the vinyl to acquaint herself with its music. Upon placing it, as she lifted the needle and set it down,

Etta James' soulful voice enveloped the room. She embraced the rhythm and moved in harmony with the singer's voice. She twirled smoothly, running her hands across the sideboard. In her wake, clouds of dust danced around her, mirroring her joyful energy.

She grasped the TV remote and climbed onto the sofa and mouthed the lyrics to At Last. Steadily, her movements grew bolder. As if in a spotlight, she continued her impromptu performance, directing it towards the figurines perched on the fireplace.

Graciously, she balanced on the sofa arm and prepared to deliver the last note with a dramatic flourish. However, just before she could let her voice soar, the distinct sound of someone clearing their throat abruptly shattered her moment.

Ru screamed and lost her balance. She tumbled backward off the sofa arm and twisted her ankle. The two intruders winced in sympathy and rushed to assist. Despite her pain, Ru, with a mix of embarrassment and pride, shooed them away, peppering them with a barrage of questions even as she clutched her throbbing ankle.

"Who are you? What are you doing here? How did you get in?"

A stout older lady stepped forward, placing her Hessian bags on the floor before addressing Ru's inquiries.

"So sorry to frighten you, dear. We didn't think you'd be here until tomorrow! We've brought you some groceries: milk, butter, eggs and bread. Lynn mentioned you used to enjoy baking bread when you were little, but it's been so long since you've been here that you've forgotten all about it. I'm sure in London you have all those fancy bakeries." Unable to contain herself, Ru interjected,

"Sorry, but once again, who are you? What are you doing here? How did you get in? Ouch, that hurts!" The man with thick auburn hair had prodded her injured foot.

"Apologies, hi. My name's Daniel," the man introduced himself. "Mrs H was offered my help with the cottage before you got here."

Ru remained silent, her gaze fixed on both of them, waiting for a more thorough explanation.

"Oh dear, did Lynn not mention anything in her letter?" inquired Mrs Harrison, or Mrs H, as she preferred to be called. "Your aunt was a close friend of mine, God rest her soul. When your mother called, it thrilled us to hear that you'd be taking over the cottage. I promised her I'd keep an eye out for you and bring some groceries to help you settle in. You won't find many takeaways around here, my dear."

Ru accepted Daniel's offer to assist her to her feet and stopped the record from skipping. She realised he was taller than her, which was a rare and pleasant surprise. His kind eyes drew her in, but a noticeable scar on one side of his nose piqued her curiosity even more. She thanked him and with a slight tilt of her head, signalled for him to explain his presence. Daniel cleared his throat once more.

"Oh, sorry, I'm kind of the handyman around here. The garden centre down Manor Lane? That's mine." He pointed out, somewhat foolishly assuming Ru was familiar with the location he mentioned. She smiled tactfully and responded,

"I'm not yet familiar with it." Then, glimpsing her reflection in a nearby mirror, she wiped away traces of yesterday's mascara. From a distance, Mrs H chimed in,

"I'll put the kettle on. I'm afraid your auntie wasn't one for drinking coffee, so you'll have to settle for tea for now. Coffee is so bad for you, you know? My Dennis cut back in 1989, and the headaches almost killed him, but he persevered and got through it," she called out, her voice echoing from the kitchen.

She exchanged a playful glance with Daniel and she rolled her eyes. Ru signalled she was going to head upstairs to change. He caught her cue and responded with a broad, understanding smile, then turned his attention to the kitchen, joining Mrs H in her efforts to unpack the groceries.

After a brief respite, Ru returned to the kitchen and was more at ease in her casual attire. In her relaxed jeans and an oversized burgundy jumper, she exuded an aura of pure comfort. Her hair was pulled up into a messy bun and she wore thick-framed glasses.

Meanwhile, Daniel had just finished tightening a screw on the cutlery drawer. He opened and closed it, ensuring its smooth movement.

"Thanks, that was on my list," she remarked with appreciation. She then turned to Mrs H, offering gratitude as she poured loose tea leaves through a strainer and into the spaniel mug. Subsequently, two more mugs emerged from the cabinet, each adorned with a different dog breed - one with a labrador and the other with a terrier.

In the meantime, Daniel was engrossed in another task. He crouched by the sink, lining up cleaning bottles and lay on his back tinkering with the pipework beneath the sink. Ru, distracted by the sight, couldn't help but steal glances at his stomach. Daniel's navy blue jumper had ridden up a tad, giving away hints of his stocky build.

"Could I get a sugar for me, please, Mrs H?" Daniel's muffled voice came from beneath the sink, to which Mrs H responded,

"You know sugar is terrible for you. Sally gave up sugar last year, and she's already shed 8 lbs." In a teasing gesture, Mrs H playfully swiped at Daniel's midriff with a flower-covered tea towel. She then shot a cheeky wink in Ru's direction, causing her to blush.

Mrs H opted for the chair with armrests. As she settled down, she busied herself with filling the empty fruit bowl with fresh apples and bananas. Seeing an opportunity to bond, she eagerly shared her cherished memories of Auntie Lynn with Ru, emphasising the long history they shared since their High School days. Mrs H broke from the reminiscence to inquire.

"What have you got planned today then, Ruth?" As she spoke, she began tidying up, clearing away the empty tea mugs. Slightly correcting her, Ru replied,

"I prefer to be called Ru. My plan is to have a bath and then go through some of Auntie Lynn's clothes." She winced noticeably when she put weight on her injured ankle. Mrs H expressed her sympathy. She then gathered her belongings and made her way to the door, adding,

"Your aunt spoke so fondly of you. She truly missed you towards the end." Ru, with a mix of sadness and defensiveness, responded,

"Auntie Lynn couldn't recognise anyone in her last days. I doubt she remembered me, especially since we hadn't seen each other for quite a while." Ru hadn't attempted to see her aunt post-diagnosis. With tears brimming, Mrs H gently countered,

"She remembered you, my dear." She pulled out a handkerchief and dabbed her eyes. Once the elderly lady left the cottage, Ru's gaze landed on Daniel, who was now busy trying to clean a mysterious substance off his jeans. She asked,

"Is everyone here like this? Thinking it's alright to just waltz into someone's home and be overly intrusive?" Ru's frustration was obvious as she hobbled across the kitchen. Daniel replied,

"Pretty much. They mean well, but yes, privacy is a luxury in Puckleworth. Need some help upstairs, Ms James?" He jabbed, a playful smirk on his face. She responded in her most exaggerated diva tone,

"No thank you, darling. I can manage my way to my dressing room. And while you're at it, please inform the venue that I won't be performing tonight." She shot him a cheeky grin, the playful energy palpable.

"But tell me, should I be prepared for an onslaught of neighbours?" Daniel shook his head.

"Lynn often left the door unlocked. Puckleworth is a sanctuary in its own right. Even though folks here are undeniably curious, they genuinely look out for one another, especially for your aunt." A trace of sadness tinted his voice, revealing deeper emotions. Ru surmised Daniel must have shared a special bond with Auntie Lynn. However, just as she was piecing thoughts together, he caught her off-guard with a pointed question:

"Why didn't you come back?"

Ru hesitated. She averted her gaze, not ready to delve into that part of her past. Wanting to divert the topic without seeming rude, she channelled her inner diva once more, using humour as her shield. She replied,

"I guess you'll have to wait for the documentary to come out, Mr?"

"Fletcher," he interjected, "Daniel Fletcher." He reached out to shake her hand. Their eyes met, and he held the gaze just a tad longer than expected, causing her to shift her eyes downward in a mix of surprise and shyness. With a knowing smile, he added,

"See you around, Ru."

Chapter Two

In the heart of the small cottage, the bathroom exuded a charming and cosy atmosphere. Importantly, despite its limited space, every inch was thoughtfully designed to maximise utility. The walls, gracefully adorned with white subway tiles, lent the room a pristine and classic aura.

A vintage pedestal sink with ornate brass fixtures claimed its spot against one wall, and right above it, a matching brass-framed mirror. Strategically placed, a petite glass shelf above the sink cradled delicate porcelain trinkets, each telling a story of its own.

The flooring featured rustic wooden planks that brought warmth and old-world character to the ambiance. As a centrepiece, the bathtub boasted a gleaming white porcelain exterior. Its inherent elegance was further amplified by the brass faucet and distinguished clawed feet. On its side, a handy wooden caddy presented an array of bath products, each whispering relaxation and indulgence.

The bathroom's endearing features were illuminated by streams of natural light that filtered in through a modest window. Ru attentively surveyed the eclectic collection of items in Auntie Lynn's bathroom. The assortment, representing a balance between delightful fragrances and practical necessities. It was a tangible representation of her aunt's singular persona.

Drawn by its familiar scent, her gaze settled on the rose-scented bubble bath. Memories stirred; Auntie Lynn had always held a fondness for her baths, discovering solace in the embrace of warm water. With reverence, Ru poured a generous dollop of the bubble bath under the cascading tap. She watched, entranced, as fluffy pink bubbles birthed and multiplied, blanketing the room in a fragrant bouquet.

While awaiting the tub to brim, Ru's attention was arrested by a new loofah, still sporting its price tag. She delicately detached the tag, allowing the loofah to kiss the water and absorb its warmth. After it was sufficiently soaked, she drizzled a modest amount of the rose-scented potion onto it. She embraced the moment and caressed her skin with the loofah. Each stroke immerses her deeper into a world of soothing comfort and cherished memories.

Whilst submerged in the fragrant bath, Ru was enveloped by the scents that triggered vivid memories. These simple, yet profound, items painted a picture of her aunt's nurturing spirit. This reminded Ru of the depth of love and care her auntie had invested in her own well-being.

She relished the moment and exhaled a contented sigh, allowing the nurturing embrace of the warm water to wrap around her, melting away the day's stresses.

Upon emerging from this therapeutic bath, something under the sink caught Ru's eye: a brass tin. She was drawn by its antiquated charm and the distinct First Aid cross engraved on it. In the light of her sore ankle, she reached out with curiosity. She cradled it in her hands and felt its reassuring weight. Inside, the tin revealed a well-organised medley of first aid essentials: various bandages, adhesive strips and a small bottle of antiseptic solution. She was flooded with warmth. Ru was once again reminded of her auntie's meticulous nature. This simple tin epitomised Auntie Lynn's ever-prepared attitude, always ready to tend to any minor scrapes or bruises that life might present.

As Ru's ankle throbbed noticeably, she quickly recognised the immediate utility of the First Aid supplies. Without hesitation, she plucked a bandage from the assortment in the tin. Carefully and tenderly, she wrapped it around her swollen ankle, securing it for a snug fit. This simple act granted her palpable relief, both in a physical sense and emotionally, tethering her to memories of being cared for.

There she was, perched on the edge of her bath, a ship adrift in an expansive sea of memories and emotions. Her mind, unbidden, steered her towards a raw, painful void that had scarred her life - her father's passing when she was very young. The subsequent years had been shadowed by her mother's grief who struggled to find a lifeline and sought solace in the bottom of a bottle most nights.

In that vast expanse of time, Ru's heart had ached for maternal affection. She had a profound sense of loss that compounded the grief of her father's passing. It was as if she had been bereft of both her father and the nurturing warmth of a mother. This led to a void in her childhood, an echoing emptiness in her heart that sought the love and affection she felt she had been denied by her mother.

Auntie Lynn tried to fill that void so when she died, a tsunami of fresh grief washed over Ru. Despite the gauntlet of challenges and the sharp sting of her emotional wounds, Ru had crafted her own path in life. She had moulded herself into a figure of resilience and independence, leaning on her internal reserves of strength to weather the storms. Yet, buried deep within her, the yearning for maternal affection persisted.

On this day, as Ru cast her gaze through the cottage window, the serene tableau of the garden offered a balm for her soul. The vibrant dance of blossoming flowers and the tender undulations of the trees whispered to her. This affirmed that, amidst the shadows of loss and yearning, lay radiant pockets of beauty and promise.

Perhaps, she mused, delving into the tales of this tranquil haven might unveil chapters of her own narrative. Maybe she'd discover those elusive pieces that would catalyse her healing and personal growth. She embraced this hope and inhaled, exhaling the weight of her musings.

Deep in thought, Ru couldn't help but contrast the rhythm of this tranquil place with the relentless hum of the bustling streets of London she had grown accustomed to.

In the vibrant heart of Hackney, she had carved a niche for herself as a florist's assistant. She'd found refuge and purpose, immersing herself in the delicate realm of flowers, all within the cosy embrace of a unique coffee and flower shop.

When the executor of her aunt's Will presented her with the deeds to Blossom Cottage, she found herself at the crossroads of a life-altering decision. She weighed her options. On one side, there lay the allure of the familiar - the pulsating energy of London and the opportunity to further hone her skills. On the other, the prospect of starting afresh in the peaceful embrace of the countryside. With the mortgage already settled and the upkeep costs being modest, the decision became tantalising.

After several introspective months, Ru took the leap. She tendered her notice both to her flat and her job, taking a definitive step away from the vibrant chaos of the city.

Her reminiscence was interrupted by a peculiar sound. She was startled by the noise and so she tuned into the tapping noise that echoed from the corridor outside the bathroom. Quickly, she dried herself off and draped a fluffy dressing gown around her, shielding her from the slight chill of the house. Straining her ears, she tried to discern the origins of the mysterious noise.

She stepped out of the bathroom, making her way down the narrow corridor, each footstep muted against the creaky wooden floorboards. As she ventured further, the tapping sound grew more pronounced, leading her towards a closed door along the passageway.

Curiosity piqued, Ru reached out and turned the doorknob, creaking the door open. The room was a study containing books on shelves, a cluttered desk, and a worn armchair. A small window allowed a sliver of sunlight to filter in, illuminating the dust particles floating in the air.

Inside the room, Ru discovered a cat perched on the windowsill, its paw tapping against the glass. How curious, she thought. She hadn't noticed a cat flap anywhere in the cottage. The cat turned its head, its bright green eyes meeting Ru's gaze. It had sleek black fur with a few scattered patches of white, giving it a distinctive and mischievous appearance.

She approached the cat, intrigued by its presence. She extended a hand, offering it a gentle pat on the head. The cat responded by rubbing against her leg and purring.

"Well, hello there." Ru spoke with surprise and delight in her voice. "I didn't know Auntie Lynn had a cat." As if in response, the cat let out a soft meow, acknowledging Ru's comment. She noticed a sense of connection to the furry creature. It resembled her neighbour's cat back in London. She'd always wanted a cat, but her landlord wouldn't allow it. However, now, the world was her oyster.

With a newfound companion by her side, Ru explored the study further. She couldn't resist the allure of the books and the intriguing stories that awaited her within those pages. She settled into the worn armchair, the soft cushioning embracing her as she picked up a book from the nearby shelf. The title caught her attention: *"Whispers of the Past: Tales from Puckleworth"*.

As she opened the book, she was transported into a world of stories. The words on the pages painted vivid pictures of Puckleworth's past, its vibrant characters and the history woven within its streets. The cat, sensing Ru's fascination, leapt onto the desk and pawed at the book. She chuckled, acknowledging the feline's shared curiosity and scratched behind its ears.

The purring background made time fly as Ru got absorbed in the stories. Each page revealed more about the town, its hidden treasures, and the lives of its inhabitants, past and present. In that study, surrounded by her auntie, a cat and the echoes of the past, Ru realised that her journey to Puckleworth held more significance than she had thought. It was not only a homecoming but also an opportunity to unearth her family's history.

A chill came over her as she realised she was still sitting in her dressing gown. She finished getting dressed and followed the cat as it led her through the corridors of the cottage. The feline moved with purpose, its tail swaying back and forth as it weaved through the familiar halls.

Soft light shone through the open kitchen door. The cat glanced back at her before slipping inside, as if urging her to step forward. She concluded the cat entered the house that way. Ru stepped out into the garden of Blossom Cottage, taking in the tranquil beauty that surrounded her. The cat slipped through a gate on the edge of the property and disappeared.

The air was crisp, carrying the promise of a new season and the vibrant colours that would soon burst forth. She inhaled, savouring the faint fragrance of blooming flowers in the distance. The blossoming trees created a canopy of pink and white along the borders of the garden. They seemed to dance in the gentle breeze, whispering secrets of renewal and growth.

A red brick pathway beckoned her forward, its rough surface worn by time and weather. She followed its meandering course, her footsteps crunching on fallen leaves and twigs. Along the way, she noticed the overgrown shrubbery that bordered the path, its tendrils reaching out as if to reclaim the space they once occupied. It added a touch of wildness and enchantment to the otherwise orderly garden.

When she reached the top corner, Ru's gaze settled on the black iron bistro table and chairs. They stood as a quiet invitation to sit, relax, and savour the beauty of nature. She imagined herself enjoying a cup of tea in the company of the singing birds, the rustling leaves, and the peaceful sounds of the nearby pond. It would be a perfect spot for contemplation and reflection.

Next to the bistro table, a patio swing swayed in the breeze. Ru sat down and surveyed the garden. She knew that within the confines of Blossom Cottage and its enchanting surroundings, she would find the peace and inspiration she had been seeking.

The contrast in pace was disarming, a welcome respite from the relentless harshness that had defined her days in London. Commotion caused time to blur and days to merge. In this new haven, everything unfolded, as if the spinning carousel had stopped.

Days unfurled in languid beauty, the moments stretching out like a sun-drenched afternoon. The hurried footsteps of the city were replaced by the gentle melodies of nature. Within this idyllic realm, she recalibrated her internal rhythm, aligning it with the unhurried pulse of her surroundings.

She moved through the garden with purpose and curiosity. When she stepped into the small shed, its wooden walls creaking under her weight. Inside, she was greeted by the sight of garden tools hanging from hooks and resting on shelves. The tools were organised by the previous owner.

Her attention was drawn to a potting shelf along one side of the shed. It housed an array of terracotta pots, gardening gloves, and a small book nestled in the corner. Ru was intrigued, so she reached for the book and opened its weathered pages.

The book contained a wealth of knowledge and handwritten notes for various flowers. Auntie Lynn had used this book as a guide, jotting down her own experiences and observations throughout the years. The pages were yellowed and delicate, evidence of countless gardening seasons spent tending to the beauties of Blossom Cottage.

Ru's fingers traced the faded ink on the pages, marvelling at the wealth of wisdom contained within. She discovered tips on soil preparation, planting techniques, and nurturing fresh flowers. Each entry was accompanied by Auntie Lynn's personal insights and reflections.

Pinned to a wooden beam was a business card that read, *'Fletcher Gardening Service'* and a number. She recalled her encounter with Daniel that morning and was eager to see him again. After seeing the overgrown garden, she knew she'd need help to get it sorted, so she removed it from the beam.

With the business card tucked in her pocket, she felt a sense of anticipation. The sight of the garden had reminded her of the task that lay ahead, and the help of Daniel's gardening service seemed like the perfect solution.

She returned through the garden, walked into the kitchen and removed the phone from the hook. She studied the numbers with a smile, feeling a newfound excitement for the journey she was about to embark on.

After a few rings, Daniel answered the call, his voice filled with warmth. Ru explained her situation and expressed her desire to enlist his services. To her delight, Daniel agreed to visit Blossom Cottage tomorrow afternoon to assess the garden and discuss the steps to bring it back to life.

Fate had brought her to Blossom Cottage, where she would not only uncover the lost connection of her Auntie Lynn but also find a companion in Daniel.

Chapter Three

Ru wrapped herself up, embracing the brisk air that tingled against her skin. The cream-coloured scarf provided a soft barrier against the cool breeze, and she relished the sensation as she ventured out into the world beyond her cottage.

She stepped onto the single track road, feeling a sense of freedom and anticipation. The road stretched ahead, lined with trees whose branches swayed in the wind. The surrounding landscape showcased the subtle signs of spring, with blossoms beginning to emerge and vibrant green hues replacing the dreary winter palette.

As she walked along the road, Ru marvelled at the picturesque scenes that unfolded around her. Fields of vibrant flowers danced in the distance, their colours painting a vivid tapestry against the backdrop of the rolling hills. The fresh scent of earth and budding foliage permeated the air and invigorated her senses.

She greeted the occasional passerby with a warm smile and a nod, exchanging small pleasantries. The locals had a friendly disposition, and Ru appreciated the sense of community that embraced this countryside setting.

Indeed, it was yet another custom she needed to acclimate to. In the bustling streets of London, people wore their burdens like invisible shields, their heads down, focused on surviving each day. But here, amidst the embrace of her new community, she sensed a profound shift in the fabric of human connection.

Gone were the anonymous faces lost in the urban maze. In this community, bad days never go unnoticed and there's always someone willing to help. Lost in her thoughts, Ru continued her walk, allowing the beauty of the countryside to guide her steps. She turned left and discovered a humble sized building.

The lively atmosphere and enticing aroma wafted from the café. Ru couldn't resist the temptation to step inside Shipman's Stores & café. The inviting scene before her hinted at a place where locals gathered for delicious food and warm conversation.

She pushed open the worn wooden door and was greeted by a chorus of cheerful chatter and the comforting scent of brewed coffee. The interior of the café exuded a rustic charm, with exposed brick walls adorned with vintage photographs and shelves lined with assorted jars and knick-knacks.

A counter displayed an assortment of pastries, homemade cakes and sandwiches. A chalkboard menu behind the counter listed an array of delectable options, from hearty breakfast platters to flavourful soups and sandwiches made with locally sourced ingredients.

The left window showcased a bountiful display of vibrant vegetables. Shipman's Stores & café took pride in offering wholesome and nourishing fare to its patrons. The dedication to quality ingredients and a farm-to-table ethos added to the allure of the establishment.

The right window displayed large farmhouse tables, giving a glimpse into the café's heart. People engaged in lively conversations over steaming mugs of coffee or enjoying hearty breakfasts that promised to start their day on a delicious note. The cheerful ambiance and the clinking of cutlery created a sense of warmth and community within the cosy space.

The staff wore cheerful smiles, their aprons adorned with the café's logo. They prepared orders with precision and care, ensuring that each dish was a testament to the café's commitment to culinary excellence.

Ru found herself drawn to a vacant table near the window, where she could observe the bustling activity. She settled into the comfortable chair, captivated by the sights and sounds that surrounded her. The clatter of dishes, the hum of conversations, and the inviting aroma of pastries created a harmonious symphony that enveloped her senses.

As she perused the menu, her taste buds awakened with anticipation. The crafted dishes showcased traditional and innovative flavours. Shipman's Stores & café offered more than just a meal - it was a place to connect and learn about Auntie Lynn's life.

With a smile on her face, Ru signalled to a friendly server, ready to embark on a culinary journey that would complement her exploration of the countryside and the long afternoon ahead.

As Ru enjoyed her hearty breakfast, she couldn't help but observe the interactions unfolding around her. Her attention was drawn to a lady at the counter who had just received her free chocolate brownie alongside her extra hot latte.

Milly the Barista received an ironed £5 note and was instructed to keep the change. She accepted the tip, her eyes lighting up with appreciation. With a sense of responsibility, she dropped the coins into the tip jar. She valued the tradition of sharing and contributing to the café's collective well-being. Ru continued to admire minor exchanges between customers, which confirmed her belief in Puckleworth's sound sense of community.

As she continued her breakfast, she savoured each bite of the delicious full English meal. This place had become a microcosm of the town itself, offering nourishment for both the body and the soul.

When she glanced towards the cast-iron fireplace, she noticed a heartwarming sight—a gentle, old collie dog named Mabel. The warmth emanating from the fireplace seemed to provide relief for the arthritis in Mabel's hind leg.

Beside Mabel sat Mr Smithson, a distinguished gentleman dressed in a three-piece tweed suit. His weathered face showed a life well-lived. In his hand, he held a plate of bacon from his own breakfast, which he shared with Mabel. The bond between them was clear, as Mr Smithson patted Mabel's head, their connection spanning generations.

Mr Smithson's attire and the hand-carved cane he leaned on held their own stories. The three-piece tweed suit spoke of timeless elegance and a connection to a bygone era. The hand-carved cane, crafted by his son in a school workshop, symbolised the bond between father and child and carried the weight of memories and craftsmanship.

This establishment held a special place in Mr Smithson's heart, much like Mabel's presence by the fireplace. It had been passed down through generations, just like the collies in his family.

In this cosy corner of the café, Ru witnessed the beauty of the interwoven stories that unfolded in Puckleworth.

Milly brought her the bill and apologised when she kept making mistakes on the credit card machine.

Ru smiled. She understood the challenges of learning new technology. She could sense Milly's nervousness and wanted to put her at ease. When Ru first joined the florist and café, she too struggled. She remembered the impatience of customers and their hurried demands echoing in her mind.

"Don't worry at all, Milly. Learning something new can be tricky, but you'll get the hang of it." As she continued her attempts to process the payment, Ru offered some encouraging words. After a couple more tries, she successfully processed the payment.

"Thank you for your patience. If there's anything else I can assist you with, please let me know." Ru nodded.

"No problem at all. You're doing a great job, and I'm sure you'll master the card machine soon. Have a wonderful day!"

Ru entered the store side of the establishment and was greeted by the familiar scent of bread. The warm atmosphere welcomed her as she began her shopping. She reached out and picked up a carton of milk from the refrigerated section, feeling the coolness of the container caress her hands. A sense of anticipation filled her as she made her way towards the coffee aisle, the distinct aroma of ground beans guiding her path.

The shelves displayed an array of coffee from different regions, enticing her with their rich aromas. She selected a bag of medium roast coffee, imagining the delightful aroma that would fill her cottage when she brewed it. She added a simple cafétiere to her shopping basket as there wasn't one in the cottage.

Next, Ru moved towards the deli section, where an assortment of homemade sandwiches, salads, and baked goods awaited her. She perused the options, looking for a light lunch to share with Daniel tomorrow. The savoury aroma of the quiches caught her attention, so she picked up a couple of them, along with a mixed green salad.

As Ru gathered her items, she couldn't help but feel a sense of satisfaction. The minor act of shopping for groceries had become an opportunity to nurture a budding friendship. With her shopping basket filled, Ru made her way to the checkout counter, where a young boy stood with a cheerful smile. He scanned the items, exchanging friendly conversation and sharing tidbits of advice on how to best enjoy the products Ru had chosen.

After completing the transaction, Ru thanked him for his help and made her way back out into the crisp air, the paper bags in her hands filled with the ingredients for a delightful lunch.

Chapter Four

Ru's steps were light and brisk as she made her way back to her cottage. The paper bags swaying in her hands. She reached up and loosened her cream-coloured scarf, allowing it to fall around her neck. The soft fabric no longer served as a shield against the cold but now adorned her like a light accessory.

She closed her eyes, enjoying the changing seasons and the warmth of the sun on her face. She adjusted her grip on the heavy paper bags just outside the bustling school, where joyful children played during recess. A ball bounced over the fence and landed in the bag.

"Excuse me, can we have our ball back, please?" A rosy-cheeked boy shouted as he attempted to climb the fence. A slender woman with blonde hair bound in a bun moved towards where the interaction was taking place.

"Finn, remember we don't talk to strangers, especially those standing at a school gate?"

She eyeballed Ru, who was taken aback by the insinuation. The woman's tight lips softened as she heard Ru's explanation and realised that she was Lynn's niece. She glanced at the ball and nodded with a faint smile.

"I see. Sorry for the misunderstanding. I'm Beth Axel. It's nice to meet you." She extended her hand in a gesture of greeting. Ru returned the smile, rebalanced her groceries and shook her hand.

"Nice to meet you, too. I apologise for any confusion. I just moved into Blossom Cottage, and I'm still getting to know the area."

Finn peered at Ru from behind his teacher's legs as they exchanged a few more pleasantries. Then, with a wave goodbye, she continued on her way back home.

As she walked through the vibrant streets of Puckleworth, Ru reflected on the encounters she had already had since her arrival. Each interaction drew her closer to the town's people and spirit. She seemed at home and connected to the community her Auntie Lynn belonged to.

After a short while, she entered her cottage and set the paper bags on the kitchen counter. Then she hung up her coat on a hook near the entrance, enjoying a sense of comfort and familiarity.

Meanwhile, the aroma of brewed coffee filled the air as Ru used her new cafétiere, the rich scent mingling with the warmth of the cottage. She moved to her nightstand and retrieved her notebook, flipping it open to a blank page. The smooth pages awaited her thoughts and plans for the garden that lay ahead.

Ru sat at a small wooden table in the study, sunlight filtering through lace curtains. Pausing, she took a moment to savour a sip of the steaming coffee, its warmth spreading through her body, invigorating her mind.

She made notes, jotting down ideas and observations about the garden. The overgrown shrubbery, the blossom trees, and the potential for transformation. She sketched rough diagrams, envisioning the layout and potential areas for flower beds, a vegetable patch, and perhaps even an intimate seating area for enjoying the outdoors.

As the afternoon wore on, she wrote and drew. The garden held so much potential, and she couldn't wait to bring it back to life, especially with Daniel's help and expertise. In fact, the collaboration between them appeared to be the perfect way to honour Auntie Lynn and create something beautiful in her absence.

As memories of her days at the florist and café in London swirled in her mind, Ru treasured the wisdom and expertise she'd garnered. A desire bubbled within her to sprinkle this knowledge in her newfound home. She stood at a crossroads, an undeniable pull towards that familiar world. The allure of sculpting beauty from flowers and offering delectable delights to grateful patrons ignited a passionate purpose in her heart.

However, she couldn't ignore the financial aspect of her new life. Even though the mortgage was taken care of and the cottage's upkeep was modest, she knew that relying on her reserves would deplete her resources. Her aunt had left her a sizable amount of money however, she wanted to give it purpose.

An idea sparked within her. Daniel, the garden centre owner, was both knowledgeable and supportive. Perhaps he had job openings or opportunities for her to explore. By doing so, working at the garden centre while she set up her own business could provide a steady income and valuable experience.

The thought of becoming her own boss, making her own decisions, and bringing her creative vision to life filled her with excitement and determination. She realised she was in a privileged position to pursue her dreams and turn them into reality.

Thus, with renewed motivation, Ru decided she would speak to Daniel tomorrow afternoon and express her interest in joining the garden centre team. She would seize this chance to learn, grow, and build a solid foundation for her future endeavours.

The pen stroked the pages and Ru's vision for the garden took shape on the pages of her notebook. Deep in her creativity, lost in her thoughts and plans, Ru smiled to herself. Her notebook served as a blueprint for the garden's future.

With the coffee cup now empty and the notebook filled with inspiration, Ru closed it, receiving a sense of accomplishment and anticipation. For the time being, she enjoyed the peaceful moments in her cottage and the budding dreams. with her notebook in hand, Ru looked out the window, her gaze resting on the overgrown garden beyond. In the bedroom, she pulled her suitcase up onto the bed and unzipped it. She noticed a folded piece of paper on the dresser, which she hadn't seen before, it read.

Ruth,
Once you've been through your aunt's clothes, let me know if there's anything you don't want. I'll find a new home for them.
Love Mrs H.

Ru paused for a moment. Her fingers tracing the words on the folded piece of paper. The reminder from Mrs H brought a mix of emotions, both nostalgia and a tinge of sadness. She was expecting her remaining belongings. In just a few days, her clothes and personal items would join her in this serene haven. Thankfully, since her London flat had come furnished, most of what she was expecting were clothes.

She refocused her attention on the dresser, opening it and sorted through the clothes. Each piece holding memories and a connection to her dear Auntie Lynn. Every touch filled her with a sense of closeness to her aunt, so she handled them with reverence.

As the afternoon wore on, she sorted through the clothing and memories flooded back. She recalled the times she had spent with Auntie Lynn. After her father died, she spent a lot of time in the cottage. Although she was very young, her memories of long weekends and holidays here were still vibrant. She couldn't remember much of him as she only had baby pictures and fragmented memories. But not with Auntie Lynn.

As she grew older, the trips became more staggered apart. Then her teenage years passed and she no longer enjoyed the games she used to play and the journey from

London seemed longer each time she visited. By the time she was in her mid twenties, the trips became once a year.

Thoughtful with each garment, Ru made deliberate decisions. Some pieces she set aside, knowing she would cherish and wear them, finding solace in their familiar touch. Others she folded and placed in a separate pile, signifying her intention to part ways with them and allow someone else to find joy in their presence.

In the process of sorting, memories intertwined with practicality. Ru considered the space in her cottage, her personal style and the sentimental value of each item. It was a delicate balance. She wanted to honour Auntie Lynn's memory while also creating a space for her own growth and new beginnings.

Once she had finished sorting through the clothes, Ru unpacked her suitcase. The remaining garments folded and organised. She made a mental note to inform Mrs H about the items she wished to re-home. She appreciated the help in finding them new owners who would love them as much as Auntie Lynn once did.

Chapter Five

In the early hours, Ru busied herself with routine tasks, aiming to make her new dwelling more like home. Auntie Lynn had transitioned to a care facility about half a year prior to her passing. Although her friends had checked in on the cottage, consistent upkeep had fallen by the wayside.

She removed various ornaments and artwork which were not to her taste and boxed them up for storage. The mattress was swapped with the second bedroom one and she measured the windows ready to order fresh curtains. Blossom Cottage was currently a shrine to her aunt and if she was to truly make it her own, then she would need to not act like she was coming back.

After shuffling the furniture in the living room, Ru was just sorting out the pantry when the distinct sound of tires crunching on gravel caught her attention, followed by a firm knock. She opened the door and was met with Daniel's towering presence occupying the entire door frame.

"I thought I'd be a gentleman today and knock." The corners of his lips pulled up.

"Hey, sorry time got away from me." She eyed up the scattered contents of the pantry. As she started gathering the tins and bottles, Daniel leaned in, offering a helping hand. He donned a flannel shirt with sleeves rolled up beneath his elbows and appeared rugged. His hair, tousled to one side, seemed like he had just raked his fingers through it in a casual gesture. His hands, notably larger than Ru's, gripped a multitude of cans at once.

As they organised the pantry, they shared snippets of their mornings. Ru, glancing at the clock, couldn't help but comment,

"It's incredible how fast this day is flying by. I picked up some lunch from the deli counter at Shipman's. Would you rather eat or stroll in the garden?"

"Let's walk and talk. I'm eager to hear what your thoughts are."

As they meandered through the flourishing garden, they exchanged dreams and visions for the space. Soon, the friendly black feline joined them, often flirtatiously rolling over to show his belly.

"That's Moss. He stays with Iris just down the lane." The ambience was enveloped in the sweet aroma of blossoms and the soft serenade of leaves, creating an atmosphere of serenity along the curving pathways. Ru showed Daniel her cherished nooks and corners, spilling her dreams for each space. With every narration, Daniel enriched the vision with his seasoned insights, constructing a symphony of ideas.

When they came across a vintage wooden bench nestled in a garden corner; they settled down. There was a palpable weight in the air as Daniel's gaze dropped.

"Why the long gap between visits to your aunt?"

With a deep sigh, Ru began recounting her story: the growing demands at home, her job's increasing responsibilities, and the widening chasm that had formed between her and Auntie Lynn. By the time Ru heard of her aunt's condition and rushed over, the illness had blurred her memories and she couldn't recognise her niece. In the haze of her disease, she lashed out, leading Ru to leave, never returning before the inevitable goodbye.

As Ru's voice quivered with raw emotion, Daniel's eyes resonated with profound understanding. He perceived the whirlpool of guilt, pain and regret that swirled within her.

"We cherished Lynn. My family has been part of this community for generations. It's unimaginable, the ordeal you endured, the dreams of reconciliation lost to time and circumstance."

"The pull between my obligations and my love for my aunt was agonising. I watched her fade away. It was heart-wrenching, especially when she couldn't recognise me. I yearned for more moments, more memories. But time is fleeting." He sensed her despair so covered her hand with his.

"Life's unpredictability often leaves us adrift. The silver lining exists in the now. Here, in Puckleworth, you have the canvas to paint a tribute to Auntie Lynn, to weave her essence into the garden's very soul."

She drew strength from his words and managed a teary smile.

"I can't revisit the past, but I can cultivate a future garden filled with her spirit."

"With your passion and your aunt's legacy, this garden will bloom with unparalleled magic. And remember, I'm right beside you, cheering you on, every step of the journey."

Back in the cosy confines of the cottage, Ru laid out a hearty lunch. Their heart-to-heart had lifted a burden from her, and with newfound clarity, she was ready to embrace her new life in Puckleworth. Daniel's presence was like a balm, exuding a warmth and ease that grounded her.

As they enjoyed the meal, Ru's gaze often found its way to Daniel. The sun-kissed lines on his face narrated tales of days spent under the open sky. His sturdy arms suggested hard work, not hours at the gym. The vibrant hue of his auburn locks caught the light, creating a mesmerising contrast with his deep green eyes. The more Ru looked, the more she realised her heart raced a touch faster in his presence.

There was an undeniable magnetic pull. She appreciated the man for his appearance and his kindness. Daniel also embodied authenticity, depth and allure.

"I've hired a new Duty Manager, so I have free time over the next month. It'll be mostly clearing and sorting as the Spring bulbs will bloom soon."

"Sounds great. I wanted to discuss something else with you. Do you have any part-time jobs at the garden centre?"

"I don't at the moment. They may have some at Shipman's. I believe one of the lads was talking about taking a gap year." Ru was briefly disappointed, but quickly rationalised it.

"Thanks for the suggestion. I'll check out Shipman's. My primary goal is to find work to cover expenses for now." Daniel looked at her, his eyes conveying a mix of understanding and sympathy.

"I wish I could help more on that front. But in terms of the garden, I'm at your disposal. And don't worry about paying me. Consider it a friendly gesture to help a neighbour out." Ru's heart swelled with gratitude.

"Thank you. That's generous of you."

The two continued with their lunch, and while the talk about work had been a slight hiccup, it allowed Ru to ponder her situation and her feelings for Daniel. She hadn't connected with anyone significantly for quite a while. Dates were more like fleeting encounters rather than something substantial.

"It's a fresh start," she mused, trying to make sense of the whirlwind of emotions. The corners of her lips turned up involuntarily. Despite the uncertainty, she was excited and curious about the future.

Chapter Six

Ru found herself seated in an elegantly furnished office directly above Shipman's bustling premises. Taking a moment to look around, she nestled comfortably into a luxuriously cushioned leather chair, situated opposite two of the town's well-known figures: Sally and Duncan.

The space was captivatingly serene, juxtaposed against the vibrant café that hummed below them. The rich, woody aroma of the old room meshed seamlessly with the unmistakable scent of coffee, which snuck in through a cracked window. It offered a picturesque view of the town, revealing the charming cobblestone streets and the continuous stream of locals and visitors.

Imposing antique bookshelves stood against the walls, their shelves heavily laden with a myriad of ancient books and framed photographs. Each item seemed to whisper tales of the long and cherished history of Shipman's, painting a vivid tapestry of the past.

The room's soft, ambient lighting, enhanced by the delicate lace curtains, perfectly illuminated the intricacies of the vintage wooden desk at its centre. Resting upon it was a gleaming old brass lamp and a glass vase, which cradled a bouquet of fresh, fragrant flowers.

Sally sat gracefully. Blonde locks were meticulously arranged, pinned up in a style reminiscent of a bygone era. Her floral dress perfectly complemented the nostalgic atmosphere of the room. In contrast, Duncan, with his thick, rugged beard, wore a faded sweater, its wear and tear suggesting it held as many tales as the store it represented.

Their chemistry was palpable. Ru instantly sensed that they weren't just co-owners; they were soulmates, partners in both business and life. Their silent exchanges, laden with fond memories and unspoken emotions, all built up to their shared journey.

"I'm aware it might seem odd to some," Sally started, the eloquence of her British accent setting her apart from the town's typical drawl, "but transitioning here from Bath was undoubtedly the most profound choice we've made. For us, Shipman's became more than just a business. It was our sanctuary, the canvas upon which we sketched our renewed dreams."

Duncan, ever the thoughtful one, nodded in assent as he poured steaming coffee from an ornate porcelain pot.

"The Shipman's, our predecessors, imparted more than a mere enterprise. They left us a legacy so we couldn't change the name. It's more than transactions and profit; it's a place with soul. Our aim, especially when introducing the café, was to create a haven where individuals could congregate, not just to make purchases, but to bond, reflect, and find a moment of peace."

Ru listened intently. She was touched by the couple's genuine commitment to preserving the essence of the establishment, while adding their own unique twist.

"Have you worked in a café before?" She sat up and cleared her throat.

"I worked at Flare, a small café in Hackney for almost two years. It harmoniously married the art of coffee brewing with floral arrangements. What started out as a serving roll eventually turned into a barista. Once it did, my mornings began with tending to our prized coffee machine. Edith, the owner, held a firm belief that a coffee machine, like any cherished instrument, required consistent care and affection to yield the finest brews. I spent a half hour each day ensuring its optimal performance."

Sally looked intrigued.

"You dedicated that much time every day?" With a chuckle, Ru confirmed.

"Indeed. It was my daily ritual. The sensation of the cold metal gradually warming, the machine's faint murmurs, and the tantalising scent of the first brew was an experience I cherished. I noticed your machine is different to the one I'm used to, however, I'm sure I'd get the hang of it in no time." She further reminisced.

"Being a barista went beyond merely serving coffee. It was about providing moments of solace and warmth to every customer. Every person who stepped through our doors brought with them a unique story, and I cherished being a part of their narrative."

Duncan, having attentively listened, inquired,

"How about the floral aspect?" Ru's face lit up.

"That was truly special. Initially, I assisted customers in selecting bouquets, but over time, my love for floristry grew. With Edith's guidance and my evening classes, I soon became proficient. Matching a latte with tulips or an espresso with roses became an art, dependent on our patrons' moods."

However, her expression darkened as she recounted,

"Just as I began envisioning a future for myself, combining my love for coffee and flowers, life took a sharp turn. The sudden news of my aunt's demise and the subsequent responsibilities upended everything." She looked directly at Sally and Duncan.

"Though my journey took an unexpected detour, my passion remains undiminished. I'm meticulous, especially with coffee machines," her voice laced with a playful undertone, "and you'll find that I'm both diligent and quick to adapt."

The meeting concluded with Sally and Duncan offering Ru a part-time position at Shipman's, a gesture she gratefully accepted. This role not only granted her financial stability but also the flexibility she sought, enabling her to continue rejuvenating her aunt's garden alongside Daniel.

"I can't emphasise enough how much this means to me. I'm eager to embark on this new journey."

"We're truly delighted to welcome you, Ru. Your dedication is clear, and that's the essence we seek in our family here. Remember, there's no need to hurry. Settle in at your pace."

Relieved and optimistic, Ru was now poised to merge the past's legacy with her dreams, ensuring they blossomed side by side in this enchanting town.

Chapter Seven

A chorus of birdsong permeated the silence as dawn broke. Ru pulled herself out of bed, which was noticeably more comfortable since swapping the mattresses. She found a pair of Auntie Lynn's gardening overalls hung in the wardrobe and thought they'd make a perfect outfit for her first day in the garden with Daniel.

The overalls, though worn at the knees, had a quality of timelessness to them. Their deep green fabric held faint stains, each a nod to dedicated days in the garden. As she pulled them on, Ru received an odd sense of connection, as though she was wrapping herself in years of memories, love and care.

As she began the intricate process of braiding her hair, she remembered the gentle touch of her aunt's fingers working through her locks. In her childhood, this house had been a sanctuary, a place where she was loved and pampered. The aroma of freshly baked cookies, the soft melodies of old records playing in the background, and her aunt's voice humming along - these were her refuge from the challenges at home.

Her mother, though loving in her own way, struggled with addiction, and mornings were hard. Ru often woke up to the sound of silence, her mother still asleep, battling the remnants of the previous night's indulgence. Those moments left young Ru feeling adrift and alone.

However, at Auntie Lynn's, mornings were different. They began with birdsong, the aroma of breakfast, and always, without fail, her aunt's loving touch as she brushed and braided Ru's hair. It was a simple act, but one that gave Ru a sense of belonging and normalcy.

Now, as she plaited her hair, she held a mix of emotions. There was a pang of loss. A hint of nostalgia for those simpler days, and a surge of determination to restore the garden to its former glory. After finishing her braids, she secured them with a pair of old hair ties. She gazed at her reflection, seeing a blend of her younger self and the resilient woman she'd become.

Tyres rolling up the gravel driveway drew her attention. She swung the front door open and was greeted by Daniel hopping out of his pickup truck that was parked underneath the oak tree. Ru squinted against the morning light, shading her eyes with one hand as the golden rays filtered through the leaves on the tree, casting dancing shadows over the driveway.

"Morning!"

Daniel called out, his voice cheerful. He was dressed in rugged jeans and a faded t-shirt that had seen better days. His tan from working long hours outside was clear, and there was a gleam in his eyes that spoke of his enthusiasm for the day's work ahead.

"Morning, Daniel." Her voice still groggy from her recent abandoned sleep. "I see you're all geared up."

"Always ready to get my hands dirty." He began pulling out various tools from the bed of the pickup: spades, trowels, a rake and a couple of watering cans. The sight of the well-worn tools evoked a sudden rush of memories for her - visions of her aunt tending to her beloved garden.

"You sure have a lot of equipment." She observed, walking towards him to help. Daniel smiled, handing her a pair of gloves.

"Every gardener's got their toolkit. And from what you've told me about this garden's history, we'll need all the help we can get."

Ru slipped on the gloves, admiring their snug fit.

"Thanks. It feels surreal to think I'll be working on the very ground Auntie Lynn once did."
Daniel's expression softened, and he put a reassuring hand on her shoulder.

"Her connection with this place was genuine. I'm sure with a bit of love and hard work, you'll bring it back to life."

The sun's rays played a game of peek-a-boo through the rustling leaves above, casting dappled light onto the flowerbeds and footpaths. Ru and Daniel worked in harmony, with him sharing his knowledge of gardening and her offering insights from Auntie Lynn's gardening journals she had discovered in the shed.

As Daniel pruned a particularly overgrown rosebush, Ru meticulously cleared a patch of land for planting. The chirping of the birds and the rhythmic sounds of their tools against the earth created a peaceful symphony punctuated by their occasional laughter and banter.

Around mid-morning, Ru fetched a tray from the kitchen. On it, she placed freshly squeezed lemonade, sandwiches wrapped in parchment paper and slices of Auntie Lynn's famous apple pie, which she had found in the freezer and thawed overnight. She carried the tray outside, placing it on a weathered garden table under the shade of a large pergola.

"Thought we could use a break," she announced, her face glistening with a thin layer of sweat and dirt smudging her cheek. Daniel wiped his brow with the back of his hand, flashing a grateful smile.

"You're a lifesaver. All this work was making me famished."

They sat opposite each other, relishing the cooling effect of the lemonade as they sipped. The sandwiches, filled with ham, cheese and a generous spread of homemade pickle, were devoured in no time. The pie, with its buttery crust and sweet filling, provided a comforting end to their little feast.

As they ate, the two exchanged stories, with Daniel recounting tales of gardens he'd worked on and Ru reminiscing about summers spent at Auntie Lynn's. They found common ground in their love for nature and the tranquil garden brought to their lives.

Post-lunch, they resumed their work with renewed energy. Ru, with a gardening fork in hand, started preparing the beds for the new saplings, while Daniel got busy fixing a trellis for a creeping jasmine plant.

By late afternoon, they had made significant progress. The garden, once forgotten and overgrown, was slowly reclaiming its former beauty. Tired yet content, they stood side by side, admiring their day's work.

"It's been a good day," Daniel remarked, stretching his back. Ru nodded in agreement.

"Thanks to you. Auntie Lynn would be so pleased."

As the sun began its descent, casting a golden hue over everything, the garden seemed to come alive, whispering secrets of the past and promises of the future.

Chapter Eight

The cream apron of Shipman's café complimented Ru's natural complexion. She arrived early so she could familiarise herself with the time cards, the staff room and of course meet her colleagues.

Milly was already behind the counter, the soft morning light streaming through the windows highlighting her curly chestnut hair. The whirring of the coffee machine and the faint aroma of freshly baked pastries filled the air. She waved excitedly when she saw Ru.

"Ru! So good to see you again. Welcome to Shipman's!" she rushed over and enveloped Ru in a warm embrace.

"Thanks, Milly. It feels great to be here." Her nervousness easing a bit with Milly's familiar and friendly face. She took Ru on a quick tour.

"Here's where we punch in and the staff room is through there. There's always a pot of coffee brewing, and stash any snacks or lunch items in the fridge."

Ru peeked into the small staff room. There was a round table with mismatched chairs, a bulletin board with various notices, and a comfy-looking couch in one corner. A few personal touches, like a potted plant on the windowsill and hand-drawn doodles on the board, made it feel welcoming.

They then headed to the kitchen. Milly introduced her to the kitchen staff, including Chef Marco who ran into the kitchen with an infectious enthusiasm, and Jenna, the young baker responsible for the café's delectable pastries. Everyone greeted Ru with smiles, and she could sense a genuine camaraderie among the staff.

"And this is your station. Espresso machine to the left, register to the right, and cappuccino straight ahead!"

The soft chime of the entrance bell rang frequently, signalling patrons eager for their morning caffeine fix.

Conversations merged into a lively hum, interspersed with the clinking of cups and the distant, rhythmic grinding of the coffee beans. Milly, with her ever-present vivacious energy, took Ru under her wing. She darted around with practised ease, her movements fluid and efficient.

"Rule number one," she handed Ru a freshly cleaned porta filter. "Always start with a clean machine. A good coffee is a product of love and a clean machine."

Ru watched in awe as Milly showed the art of tamping the coffee grounds - applying just the right amount of pressure to ensure a smooth and consistent shot.

"It's all in the wrist." She advised with a wink.

Under Milly's expert guidance, Ru got back up to speed with the intricacies of the espresso machine. Although she was rusty after her time off, the once intimidating array of buttons and levers soon became familiar tools in her hands. Milly's teachings went beyond mere technique. She instilled in Ru the importance of the ritual, the dance of being in sync with the machine, and the delicate balance between precision and intuition. Frothing milk was next on the agenda.

"You're aiming for velvety microfoam," Milly instructed, demonstrating the correct angle to hold the steam wand and the gentle hissing sound to listen for. Ru practised diligently, delighting in the transformation of cold milk into a warm, creamy texture that melded seamlessly with the espresso.

The first cappuccino Ru crafted, under Milly's watchful eyes, demonstrated her swift learning on this machine. The rich espresso settled at the bottom, topped with a luxurious layer of froth, crowned with a sprinkle of cocoa. As she handed it over to a waiting customer, the appreciative nod she received filled her with a sense of accomplishment.

Throughout the morning, Ru was introduced to regulars, each with their unique orders and quirks. There was Joe, who insisted on a double shot of espresso with a hint of caramel, and

Mrs Alvarez, who loved her lattes extra frothy with a dash of nutmeg.

"Ruth!" called out an elderly gentleman with a mane of white hair and twinkling blue eyes. "You're Lynn's niece, aren't you? I'm so sorry about your loss. She was a good friend of mine."

"Thank you, sir. It's nice to meet you."

"Call me George. Everyone does."

Between serving customers, Milly shared snippets of café lore with Ru, from the tale of the couple who got engaged right at the corner table to the time a famous actor had popped in for a quick espresso shot. As the hours ticked by, Ru developed an increasing connection to the café. The rhythm of the work, the warmth of the regular customers, and the camaraderie with Milly made her seem right at home.

By the end of her shift, her feet ached, and her hands bore the telltale signs of a barista – a few splashes of milk and a smudge of cocoa. But her heart was light. The day was filled with new experiences and connections. As she hung up her apron, she acknowledged a surge of gratitude.

Chapter Nine

The sun hung low in the sky, casting a warm golden hue over the expansive garden. This once-forgotten piece of land, a tangle of brambles and nettles interspersed with the remnants of old flowerbeds, was slowly resembling the sanctuary Ru envisioned.

With her hair tied back into a messy bun and a faded sun hat perched atop her head, she was engrossed in her task. She meticulously cleared an area of its thorny weeds, revealing the dark, fertile soil beneath. Now and then, she'd unearth an old flower bulb, long dormant but still brimming with life, waiting for its chance to bloom once more.

Daniel worked a short distance away. His brow furrowed in concentration as he meticulously assembled a rustic wooden trellis, destined to become the backbone for fragrant climbing roses and starry jasmines. His toolbox lay open nearby, its contents scattered about. Ru's hands, although gloved, were streaked with earth, her face smudged with a mix of sweat and dirt.

"Imagine," she began, catching her breath, "in a few months, this spot right here will be a riot of colours - blues, pinks, yellows. It'll be like my very own Monet painting."

Daniel teasingly brandished a tomato seedling like a trophy.

"And over there, behind the rose archway, you'll have a treasure trove of veggies. Fresh salads every day!"

Their interactions were punctuated by laughter, playful banter and the occasional water fight using their gardening cans. They discovered relics from the garden's past life – a sun-bleached garden gnome with a chipped hat, a once-vibrant ceramic bird bath now housing a tiny ecosystem, and a stone plaque, slightly moss-covered, that read, *'Bloom where you are planted.'*

As the day wore on, they mapped out spaces for various plants. Ru envisaged a corner that paid homage to her aunt, teeming with old-fashioned roses, lavender and peonies. Daniel, ever the dreamer, spoke of a secluded nook, its boundaries marked by tall bamboo shoots and a carpet of ferns, ideal for meditation and reflection.

By the time twilight approached, a symphony of evening sounds emerged. Crickets started their chorus, and in the distance, an owl announced its presence. Sitting side by side on an old stone bench, they gazed upon their day's work. The garden was far from complete, yet the changes were clear - patches of cleared earth ready for seeds, the sturdy trellis awaiting its climbers, and pathways outlined with string.

As she woke on the last day of her second week, she texted Daniel and asked if they could take a day off. Her body was bearing the strain from her new job and intensive gardening.

She ambled down Willow Lane and made her way towards the high street. The charm of Puckleworth lay not just in its scenic beauty but also in its quaint establishments. Every shop reflected the soul of the town. Ru relished the unhurried pace of the afternoon, soaking in the sights and sounds of her new home.

The bookshop was a particular delight. Nestled between a hairdresser and a florist, its wooden sign read *"Thistle & Quill."* The bell above the door chimed delicately as Ru entered. The warm, musty scent of old books filled the air. Rows upon rows of wooden shelves lined the walls, each filled with volumes ranging from worn-out classics to gleaming new releases.

A reading nook sat by the window with a plush armchair and a floor lamp. Ru spent a good few hours there, flipping through pages of poetry, historical fiction, and even a gardening guide or two.

Next, she wandered into a gift shop called *"Puckle Treasures."* Handmade jewellery, fragrant candles, artisanal soaps and quirky knick-knacks filled the space. A delicate silver necklace with a pendant shaped like a willow tree caught her eye. It reminded her of Willow Lane. The friendly shop owner, an older woman with spectacles perched on her nose, wrapped it up in a small velvet box after Ru treated herself.

Her next stop was the butcher's, named *"Goodfield's Prime Cuts."* Though she needed nothing, the display of fresh produce and the energetic banter between the butcher and his customers drew her in. She left with some advice on preparing a roast and a promise to return.

The tool shop, a no-nonsense establishment called *"Hartwell's Hardware,"* had a window display of gardening tools. Given her recent endeavours in the garden, Ru took a keen interest in the selection. She chatted with Mr Hartwell, a stout man with hands as rough as bark, about garden shears and soil testers.

Ru retraced her steps down the high street, her purchases in hand. There was a deeper connection to Puckleworth now, understanding its rhythms and nuances better. Each shopkeeper, each conversation, each smile shared added another layer to her burgeoning relationship with the town. And as she passed the charity shop, she saw her aunt's dress Mrs H had donated, displayed so prominently. There was a comforting sense of continuity, a bridge between the past and her future here.

When she returned to her cottage, she found Mrs H sat in her car on the gravel drive. Ru knocked on the window softly, which disrupted Mrs H's podcast in her headphones.

"Hey, were you after me?" Ru poked her head over the opened car door.

"Yes, I wanted to see how you're doing? I've been cat sitting the past few days."

"Come on in. I'll pop the kettle on."

Ru opened the door to her cottage, the comforting aroma of her earlier breakfast still faint in the air. As she prepared the tea, Mrs H settled into one of the dining chairs, her eyes roving around the room with keen interest.

"These bags... what goodies did you find today?" she inquired with a twinkle in her eyes, pointing at the assortment of bags Ru had placed on the kitchen counter.

"Just a few things from the high street shops," Ru grinned. "A necklace from Puckle Treasures, a book from Thistle & Quill, and some advice on roasting from Goodfield's."

"I'm fond of Thistle & Quill myself. Their mystery section is quite riveting."

The kettle whistled, signalling that the water was ready. Ru prepared two cups, adding a dash of milk to her guest's as she remembered from their last meeting. As they sipped their tea, Mrs H leaned forward, her expression turning more serious.

"I wanted to check on you, dear. Losing someone is never easy, and diving straight into work and this gardening project with Daniel might be taxing."

Ru looked down, swirling the tea in her cup.

"It's been... a whirlwind. But the garden, this house, and even the job at Shipman's – they all help. They connect me to Auntie Lynn." Mrs H nodded.

"That's a beautiful sentiment. And it's important to remember to give yourself space to grieve and to rest." Ru smiled and was comforted by Mrs H's words.

"I actually took today off from gardening."

"That's a wise decision." Mrs H patted Ru's hand. "Remember, Puckleworth is not just buildings and streets. It's a community. And we're here for you."

Gratitude washed over her. In just a short time, she'd found genuine connections in this little town – from the kind-hearted shopkeepers to the ever-supportive Mrs H.

Afternoon came and she browsed the internet for garden furniture, ready for when summer arrived. As she scrolled, an advert directed her to the local garden centre owned and ran by Daniel. She curiously clicked on the *"About Us'"* page and studied the history.

A picture showed Daniel, his sun-kissed face stressed with a few flecks of dirt, a testament to his hands-on approach in the garden. He stood against a backdrop of vibrant flowers and lush greenery, his genuine smile radiating warmth. There was a twinkle in his eyes, revealing the passion he held for his work.

The page detailed the history of the garden centre:

Established in 1989 by the Morgan family, the Puckleworth Garden Centre has been a cherished landmark for over three decades. Originally a small nursery selling local plants and seeds, the centre quickly grew in popularity under the guidance of Leonard Morgan, who saw a sanctuary for both plants and people.

In 2005, his grandson, Daniel Morgan, took the helm. With a degree in Horticulture and a natural flair for landscaping, Daniel transformed the centre into a haven for gardening enthusiasts. The Puckleworth Garden Centre, under his leadership, offered not only a wide variety of plants but also organic gardening supplies, and custom landscaping solutions.

Our philosophy is simple: 'Nature and nurture.' We believe in cultivating plants with care, offering our customers the best products, and giving back to the community. Our team, led by Daniel, is dedicated to ensuring every visitor leaves with a smile, a plant, or perhaps both!

Ru found herself immersed in the narrative, captivated by the story behind the garden centre she had only known through

Daniel's involvement in her own garden. The dedication and hard work it took to run such an establishment were palpable. It gave her a deeper appreciation for Daniel's expertise and commitment.

Ru navigated to the garden furniture section. Beautiful wooden benches, elegant ironwork chairs and vibrant outdoor cushions greeted her. She recognised the quality firsthand which made her more confident making a selection from Daniel's centre.

There was something about him that intrigued her. Beyond his obvious knowledge and passion for gardening, there was a depth to him. A sincerity that resonated whenever he spoke of plants, of life, of memories embedded in the soil. He had this way of making the world around them come alive, making her see things she'd never noticed before. But it wasn't just that.

Every gesture, every shared augh over a gardening joke, every time their hands brushed when passing a tool – they left an indelible mark on her. She looked forward to their gardening sessions, not just for the progress they made in the garden but for those stolen moments of connection.

Daniel had an old-fashioned charm. His laughter was hearty, and his manners were impeccable. He treated her, and everyone around him, with respect and kindness. She understood his popularity as both a skilled gardener and a person. She shook her head and laughed to herself. She mused.

"It's been two weeks, Ru. Get a grip!" But even as she thought it, she couldn't deny the little flutter in her stomach or the warmth that spread across her cheeks. It had been a while since she felt this way. She was both excited and apprehensive about the growing connection.

She closed the laptop lid and headed outside to take a moment to breathe in the fresh air. The garden was coming alive, bit by bit, day by day. And so, it seemed, was something blossoming inside her. The future was uncertain, but for now, she embraced the journey, wherever it might lead.

Chapter Ten

Shipman's was busy this morning. Ru helped Milly rearrange the tables for a group booking that was due at 10am. They religiously came every Tuesday morning. Ru watched as the women from the knit and natter group arrived. Some shuffled in slowly, leaning on walking sticks or supporting each other's arms, while others entered with brisk strides, knitting bags swinging by their sides. Each one greeted Milly and Ru with bright smiles, expressing their appreciation for the thoughtfully arranged tables.

Iris, the owner of Moss and the group's coordinator, was the last to arrive. A spry woman in her seventies with silver hair neatly tied in a bun, she was the heartbeat of the knit and natter group. Her fingers danced with expertise and grace, weaving yarn into intricate patterns even as she chatted animatedly with those around her.

"Morning, Ru! Thanks for setting up the tables this way. Makes it easier for all of us to chat and share," Iris beamed at her. Ru smiled back.

"Of course. Anything for the knit and natter group. How's the baby blanket project coming along?"

"Oh, splendid." Her eyes twinkled. "We're almost at our target. The hospital will be thrilled. These blankets will provide comfort to many newborns and their families."

As the morning progressed, the café was filled with the rhythmic clicking of knitting needles, bursts of laughter, and an endless stream of stories. The women shared tales from their youth, discussed current events, and even exchanged recipes. Every once in a while, one of them would hold up their work, seeking feedback or proudly displaying a tricky pattern they'd mastered.

Ru found herself drawn into their world. During a brief lull in her tasks, she approached the group with a coffeepot in hand, ready to offer refills. On a whim, she asked,

"Would you mind showing me a few basic stitches? When things calm down of course." Iris looked up with a delighted smile.

"Of course, dear! We'd be happy to have another pair of hands join our project."

The rest of the morning passed in a blur, with Ru picking up the basics of knitting under the patient guidance of the group. By the end of her shift, she'd produced a small, albeit wonky, square. The women cheered her on, promising that with time, her squares would be as neat as theirs.

As Ru watched them leave, bags filled with multi coloured yarns and half-finished squares, a warmth spread in her chest. The day drew to a close so Milly and Ru closed up. They dutifully lifted the chairs, swept and mopped the floor.

"Lynn used to be part of this group. I miss her so much. She knitted me this cardigan." Milly pulled out a mustard yellow chunky knit cardigan from her bag. "Was she your aunt on your mum's side or your dad's?"

"Mum's. She's actually my great aunt. Mum's an only child." Ru continued the tidying up.

"Are you close?"

Ru's gaze shifted downwards.

"Not really no, mum has… well she has… it's complex." She stumbled over her words, not feeling too comfortable discussing the history with Milly. Sensing her shift in tone, Milly continued.

"Sorry I didn't mean to pry."

"Not at all. I don't speak to mum too often and when I do, things often get heated, so I stay away. I've tried over the years to reconcile however, she can be unpredictable."

Milly picked up her cardigan then looked at Ru.

"Family dynamics can be so complicated," she breathed, her voice filled with understanding. "It's not always black and white. These types of relationships have numerous layers."

Ru leaned against the counter, a sigh escaping her lips.

"Yeah, it's just... I wish it was different. I wish we could have that bond everyone talks about. But it's like we're on two different wavelengths. I thought coming here, handling Auntie Lynn's estate would give us a common ground, but...," she shrugged helplessly.

Milly reached out, placing a comforting hand on Ru's arm.

"It's okay, Ru. You're doing what's best for you. It's essential to take care of your mental and emotional well-being. Sometimes, distance is necessary."

Ru nodded, brushing away an unexpected tear.

"I missed having that mother-daughter connection, you know? When I saw it with Auntie Lynn, I could see her genuine care and constant presence. I craved that."

"You've got so much strength in you, Ru," Milly eyes glittering with sincerity. "It's commendable that you took the step to come here. Know you've got a family here too."

Ru smiled weakly.

"Thanks, Milly. It means a lot to hear that."

"Anytime. We're here for each other."

The room was filled with a comfortable silence as the two continued with their closing tasks. The burdens a little lighter, and the evening a little brighter, knowing they had each other's support.

Chapter Eleven

The day dawned clear and bright, and Ru found herself with an unexpected free day. The idea of staying indoors was almost like a waste, so she visited Daniel's garden centre, a place she had heard so much about but had never seen firsthand. After she pulled on her favourite blue dress and laced up her white sneakers, she set off with an air of anticipation.

On her approach, the scent of fresh flowers, potting soil, and the sweet tang of greenery filled the air. It wasn't just a typical nursery; it was a verdant paradise nestled within the town. Stretched out over several acres, the garden centre boasted a myriad of flora ranging from the commonplace to the exotic.

Daniel was at the back, engrossed in repotting some vibrant orchids. Hearing footsteps, he looked up, his face breaking into a broad smile at the sight of Ru.

"Didn't expect to see you here on your day off!" He wiped his hands on a cloth.

"Neither did I, but the day was too beautiful to stay indoors. Plus, I've been curious about this place. Show me around?"

Daniel was more than happy to oblige. They began in the greenhouse, a vast structure made of glass and metal, where tropical plants thrived. He showed her delicate ferns, ornate bromeliads and a collection of rare orchids, each one more stunning than the last. He explained the intricacies of their care, from the precise amount of sunlight to the specific humidity levels.

From there, they ventured to the outdoor sections, where rows of flowering plants danced in the wind. Bees buzzed busily, moving from one bloom to the next. Ru was particularly taken by a patch of vibrant peonies, their stunning heads turned towards the sun.

Continuing their exploration, Daniel led Ru towards another section that was nestled just beyond a stand of tall bamboo.

"You might find this area interesting," his chest boasting with pride.

As they entered, Ru was greeted by a visually stunning array of garden furniture and homeware. Elegant wrought iron benches sat beside chic wooden patio sets, each designed to transform any garden into a relaxing haven. There were hammocks with intricate patterns, loungers perfect for sunbathing, and even gazebos that promised shade on hot summer days.

"I always believe that a garden isn't just about the plants," Daniel explained, observing Ru's awestruck expression. "It extends one's home, and these pieces help in merging the indoors with the outdoors seamlessly."

Ru ran her fingers over a mosaic-topped table, its tiles catching the sun and sparkling.

"This is beautiful," she imagined the piece in her garden, laden with fresh lemonade and books. The homeware section was no less intriguing. There were ceramic pots in every hue, ornate birdhouses that would attract the most discerning of avians, and even decorative watering cans that were as functional as they were beautiful.

Just beyond, an entire section was dedicated to gifts. There were handcrafted wind chimes, delicate garden angels and a variety of seed packets tied with ribbons. Scented candles with fragrances like 'Midnight Jasmine' and 'Rose Dawn' sat next to ornate lanterns. There were also journals with botanical covers, perfect for keeping gardening notes, and kits for creating fairy gardens.

Daniel pointed out a set of hand-painted garden stones with inspiring quotes.

"These are a hit! Especially for those who want to give something memorable to gardening enthusiasts."

Ru picked up a stone that read, "Let love grow," and smiled. The duo spent a considerable time in this section, with Ru making mental notes for future purchases. The blend of utility and aesthetics in the furniture, the charm of the homeware, and the thoughtfulness of the gifts section had left a lasting impression on her.

As they strolled, Daniel shared tales of the garden centre – from the challenges of procuring rare seeds to the joy of seeing a plant bloom for the first time. He showed her the water feature section, with its serene fountains and koi ponds, and the ornamental section, filled with unique garden statues and wind chimes that sang gentle melodies.

They took a break at the garden centre café. Tucked under a canopy of grapevines, it was an intimate nook that served herbal teas and fresh baguettes - always accompanied with chunky chips or salad.

As they continued their leisurely walk through the garden centre, amid conversations about plants and furniture, Ru had a sudden thought.

"You know, Daniel," she began, inhaling the fragrant lavender, "you've shown me so much of your world here and introduced me to the art of creating a perfect garden haven."

"It's a joy sharing what I love."

Ru looked up, her eyes shining with an idea.

"How about you experience a bit of my world? I'd love for you to come by Shipman's. You can see me in action and let me know how my latte art is coming along."

Daniel's eyes lit up with interest.

"I've been there a few times in the past, but it's been a while. And I've heard about the changes and the new café section. I'd love to see it, especially with you as the guide." They both shared a moment of mutual understanding. Just as Daniel had opened up his world to Ru, she wanted to reciprocate, sharing a piece of her life.

"How about this Friday? We're having a live music evening once a month. I suggested it to Sally and Duncan who loved that idea. I used to visit somewhere that did a similar thing back in Hackney. The café has a unique charm in the evening. Dim lights, soft music, hot drinks rather than alcohol… it's quite different."

Daniel's grin grew wider.

"Sounds perfect."

Their bond, already strong because of shared interests and moments, deepened further with this exchange. Both recognised that sharing one's passion and space was a genuine gesture of trust and friendship.

The day passed in a contented blur, and by the time Ru left, she had a bag filled with new trinkets and countless ideas for her garden. More than the purchases, however, she cherished the time spent with Daniel.

Chapter Twelve

The ambiance at Shipman's was different that evening. There was an air of anticipation, a palpable excitement that hummed in harmony with the preparations for the debut live music evening.

Ru had been busy all day. She wanted everything to be perfect and she knew, as it was her initiative so her boss's eyes would be on her. The mason jars she had bought from the garden centre were strategically placed around the café. When lit, the fairy lights inside them cast a warm, ethereal glow, illuminating the delicate artificial flowers that peeked out from within. The result was enchanting; every table seemed to hold its own miniature galaxy, bathing guests in a soft luminescence.

The wooden stage, set up at one end of the café, was adorned with a similar theme. Larger jars lined its edge, interspersed with potted ferns and ivies, creating an intimate atmosphere for the performer. The old brick walls of Shipman's seemed to absorb this light, reflecting it back in a muted golden hue, adding to the room's cosy ambiance.

Guests began arriving in small groups. The familiar hum of Shipman's was now punctuated with eager whispers, the clinking of mugs, and the soft strumming of the guitarist as he did his soundcheck. It was a sensory delight.

Daniel walked in just as the sun was setting, casting a soft orange-pink glow through the café's large windows. He looked around, clearly impressed, his gaze lingering on the mason jars.

"You've truly transformed this place." She leant close so she could hear him over the growing din. Ru, dressed in a simple black dress, smiled, her eyes shining with pride.

"I had a little inspiration," she winked, referencing their day at the garden centre.

Hushed tones emerged as the guitarist took the stage. His soulful tunes, ranging from soft ballads to upbeat folk songs, resonated with the audience. People tapped their feet and sang along. The café pulsed with life and rhythm like it hadn't before. As the last notes of a soulful ballad resonated through the café, the guitarist announced a short intermission. The audience erupted in polite applause, and the buzz of conversations resumed, intermingled with praises for the performance.

Amidst this, Ru noticed Sally motioning for her from the back of the room, near the entrance to the kitchen. Navigating her way through the sea of tables, Ru approached, curiosity clear in her eyes. Sally, always the embodiment of grace, had a fresh look tonight - one of nostalgia.

"Ru," she began, her voice softer than usual, "seeing you here, shaping this café, bringing in so much life... it reminds me so much of your Auntie Lynn."
Ru's heart caught in her chest.

"I knew Lynn very well," Sally continued. "Tonight, seeing the café brimming with life, music and laughter. I think, somewhere, she's looking down and feeling incredibly proud." Ru, overwhelmed with emotion, sensed a tear roll down her cheek.

"Thank you." Ru's voice choked with emotion. Sally nodded, pulling Ru into a comforting embrace.

The intermission came to a close as the sounds of the guitar tuning floated in the background. The two women returned to their respective roles, their bond deepened, and the weight of legacy adding layers to the magic of the evening.

The live music evening turned out to be a resounding success. Guests left with smiles on their faces, praising the ambiance, the music, and, of course, the enchanting décor. Ru and Daniel, seated at a corner table with their drinks, shared a contented look.

"Can I give you a lift back home?" He swung his coat across his shoulders.

"That would be great."

The night was thick with silence, punctuated only by the occasional distant hum of passing vehicles. Inside the car, the atmosphere was heavy, dense with unspoken words and shared memories. The soft yellow lights from the cottage filtered through the windows, casting a warm glow on the interior. Ru glanced over at Daniel, whose eyes were fixed on the steering wheel.

The car, which had served as their refuge for the past few hours, now held the depth of their conversation. Empty coffee cups, remnants from their evening, sat in the holders. The radio, which had been playing in the background, was now silent, as if giving them space to reflect.

They had covered an expanse of topics – from their individual dreams and aspirations to shared memories of the garden and the café. At moments, their laughter had filled the car, echoing stories of shared mischief and light-hearted moments. At other times, the weight of deeper confessions and vulnerabilities had rendered them silent, each lost in their thoughts.

Daniel finally broke the silence, his voice soft as he turned to face her, his eyes searching hers.

"I've never been this open with anyone. Tonight, sharing these stories, these dreams... it feels like a turning point."
Ru's heart fluttered at his words, sensing the depth of the emotion behind them.

"Me too."

Despite the late hour, they remained in the car, unwilling to end their conversation. They continued to talk, delving into stories of their pasts, hopes for the future, and everything in between.

As dawn painted the sky with hues of pink and gold, they realised they'd talked through the night. Exhausted but content, they shared a smile of understanding as Ru got out and waved at him from her front door. Daniel sighed as he turned the key, and the engine purred to life.

Chapter Thirteen

The sun was already high in the sky when Ru finally stirred from her slumber. Her bedroom was bathed in a gentle, warm light, filtered through the soft drapes. For a moment, she lay there, cocooned in her sheets, savouring the rare luxury of a slow morning. The memories of the previous night's conversation with Daniel lingered, bringing a soft smile to her lips.

After a leisurely brunch comprising scrambled eggs, toast and a steaming mug of coffee, Ru was rejuvenated. She glanced around her living room and contemplated how the house bore years of wear and tear. One task she had set for herself was to bring a fresh coat of paint to the living room walls. Today was the perfect day to embark on that task.

She pulled her hair into a messy bun and wearing her oldest pair of jeans paired with a worn-out t-shirt, Ru set the stage. The living room was soon scattered with paint cans, brushes and drop cloths. The windows were flung open, letting in the gentle breeze and the chirping of the birds outside.

She decided on a soft shade of cream with hints of peach, a colour that would bring warmth and brightness to the room. As she started, the brush strokes seemed therapeutic, a rhythmic dance between the brush, paint and the wall. Each stroke brought new life. With the music playing in the background, time seemed to flow in sync with the melodies. The tracks shifted from upbeat tunes to soulful ballads, and Ru found herself lost in the rhythm of painting and the world of the songs painted in her mind.

By late afternoon, as the golden hour approached, the transformation was clear. The walls, once stained and dull, now gleamed with a fresh coat of paint. The room was lighter, airier, and full of potential. Exhausted but satisfied, Ru rinsed out her brushes, admiring her handiwork. The paint job was not just a cosmetic change; it was symbolic. Just as she was breathing new life into her surroundings, she was also rediscovering herself, layer by layer. As she collapsed onto her couch, she took a moment to bask in the satisfaction of a job well done.

Later that night she began to feel the works of her labour so ran herself a bath. It was a luxurious affair. Ru poured in a generous amount of lavender-scented bath salts, watching as they dissolved and turned the water a milky shade of purple. The aroma of lavender, known for its calming properties, filled the air. All the aches and weariness of the day seemed to melt away. For a while, all she did was close her eyes and let her mind drift. The gentle lapping of water against the tub played like a tranquil lullaby.

Refreshed and wrapped in a fluffy robe, Ru decided it was the perfect evening for a movie night. The house still had many undiscovered treasures, and one of them was an old TV she had stumbled upon in the spare room. She set it up in her bedroom atop the wooden dresser ensuring it was still in working condition. A soft glow illuminated the screen and sent a tinge of nostalgia through her mind. It had been ages since she had indulged in a movie night, especially one in bed.

She quickly rummaged through her collection of DVDs, many of which she had brought along from her previous home. Tonight, she decided to watch something timeless. Her fingers brushed over a classic: *"Breakfast at Tiffany's"*. Audrey Hepburn's charm, the New York setting, and the iconic music was just right for the evening.

With the movie decided, Ru headed to the kitchen. She popped some corn kernels in the microwave, revelling in the staccato pops as they transformed into fluffy popcorn. After transferring them into a large bowl and seasoning them with a dash of salt and melted butter, she then grabbed a bag of crisps and an assortment of dips. A chilled soda from the fridge added the finishing touch to her movie snack ensemble.

She climbed back into bed, surrounded by cushions and her treats spread around her, Ru pressed play. As the opening credits rolled, and the familiar notes of "Moon River" filled the room, a wave of contentment washed over her.

The soft glow of the screen, the comfort of her bed, and the decadence of her snacks made the evening mood incredibly special. It was a reminder that sometimes, amidst the chaos and challenges of life, all one needed was a simple evening of indulgence and the timeless magic of cinema to be whole again.

Chapter Fourteen

On her days off from the café, Ru and Daniel, energised by the shared vision, tackled the unruly green canvas that surrounded Blossom Cottage. The process, though arduous, became a dance of collaboration and understanding. Where Ru hesitated, unsure of a plant's purpose, Daniel's expertise would shine through. And when Daniel was on the verge of discarding a seemingly unimportant shrub, Ru's sentimental memories would interject, sharing stories of Auntie Lynn and the cherished moments they held.

Mornings usually began with a cup of coffee in the kitchen, where they'd discuss the plan for the day. Daniel often arrived with fresh pastries, which became their routine treat during breaks. Ru would occasionally surprise him with homemade sandwiches or her signature lemonade, perfect for the midday break.

Their hands became weathered and stained from the earth, but the results were clear as each patch of land they cleared revealed the underlying beauty of Auntie Lynn's original garden. Ru unearthed hidden gems - old rose bushes that had been smothered by weeds, or forgotten bulbs that promised vibrant blossoms soon.

As the days melted into each other, their conversations meandered into more personal territories. Ru learned about Daniel's childhood, his dream of one day owning a large nursery, and the story behind his deep bond with nature. She shared tales of her city life, the pressures and the pace, and the longing she always wanted for a simpler existence.
In the sunset's shade, they often shared more than gardening tales. They laughed over shared stories, comforted each other during vulnerable moments, and celebrated minor victories, like

the resurrection of an old lavender bush or the discovery of a hidden pond.

The physical transformation of the garden mirrored the evolution of their relationship. The wild, untamed foliage took on a structured beauty, just as the initial hesitations and formalities between Ru and Daniel gave way to genuine affection and trust. The next day their morning was interrupted by Mrs H who had returned from a trip.

"Wow - what a difference you've made. You've worked so hard, I can't quite believe the transformation." She waddled into the cottage and returned with a tray of hot refreshments and treats.

"Perfect timing Mrs H, I'll just wash up."
Mrs H peered over her glasses at Ru, who was running her hands under the garden hose herself. She smiled at Ru knowingly.

"How are you settling in, my dear?"

"Yes, great thanks. I'm finding my way around the neighbourhood. I met Iris the other day and, of course, you'll know Moss, the cat who likes to visit. Daniel has been very helpful. I honestly couldn't have done this without him."

Mrs H was about to open her mouth and make a remark about the tangible tension she could feel between the pair when Daniel emerged from the cottage. He ducked his head as he came back outside.

"Ah, Daniel! There you are." Her eyes twinkled with mischief. "I was complimenting your incredible work here." Daniel wiped his hands on a cloth.

"Thanks. It's been quite a journey, but I'm glad we've made such progress."
Mrs H, never one to miss an opportunity for playful teasing, remarked,

"Oh, I'm not just talking about the garden." She gave Ru a sly wink, which caused her to blush and glance down at her shoes.

Aware of Mrs H's penchant for being a matchmaker and her keen observational skills, Daniel tried to steer the conversation back to safer grounds.

"Your trip to Edinburgh must have been wonderful. How's the new grandchild?"

Mrs H beamed at the change of topic, always happy to talk about her family.

"Oh, he's just adorable! A proper little cherub. Although, the city's hustle and bustle has left me yearning for the quiet of our town." Ru, grateful for the diversion, pitched in,

"There's nothing quite like the tranquillity of the countryside is there? A new family member is a blessing. I'm glad you had a good time."

As the trio sipped their tea and nibbled on the treats Mrs H had brought, they exchanged stories and news from around the village. The older woman's presence was a comforting reminder of the tight-knit community spirit. When it was time for her to leave, Mrs H stood up, leaning on her cane.

"I'll leave you two to it, then. Remember, the barn dance is next month of the 8th. The Friends Committee runs an annual fundraiser. This year funds are going towards the church roof. It'll be a wonderful opportunity for you to meet more folks, Ru. And I'm sure Daniel would be more than happy to accompany you." She gave another one of her knowing winks as she made her way down the garden path.

Ru and Daniel exchanged amused glances. Both had grown fond of Mrs H's playful nature and her not-so-subtle nudges. As the afternoon sun cast a warm golden hue over Blossom Cottage, the two resumed their work, their camaraderie only deepened by their shared interactions with the village's most spirited resident.

Chapter Fifteen

On her way to work one morning, Ru tied her shoelace outside of the primary school. Beth, the year 3 teacher swiftly came to the gates and grabbed her attention.

"Ru, good morning. I wonder if you're free tomorrow for a walk?"

She was pleasantly surprised by her invitation. Beth had been quite frosty to her on her first morning in Puckleworth.

"Yes, I am actually. I start work at 1 o'clock, but I can certainly meet you beforehand."

"Great, is 10am outside the Post Office ok?"

"Sounds great. I'll see you then - oh and wear walking boots, too."

Ru hesitated as she didn't have any, but she recalled she saw some of her aunt's in the under the stairs cupboard.

"Sure, I'll wear them." Ru hoped Auntie Lynn's boots would fit her.

After their brief exchange, Ru continued on her way to Shipman's. Her mind, however, was abuzz with curiosity. Why had Beth's demeanour towards her changed so suddenly? Their initial encounter had been nothing short of chilly, and this sudden warmth was unexpected. Maybe she had misjudged Beth, or perhaps the village's tight-knit community had their own way of warming up to newcomers.

The rest of her shift at Shipman's was its usual blend of busyness and the pleasant hum of customers, but Ru found her mind drifting back to the upcoming walk with Beth. She was eager to explore more of Puckleworth's picturesque landscapes and, hopefully, get to know her better.

The next morning, Ru woke up with a sense of excitement. She scrambled around in the under-stairs cupboard in search of footwear. There, pushed towards the back, was a pair of well-worn but sturdy walking boots. They seemed to be about her size. She took them out and examined them — they were of good quality, dusty from disuse but otherwise in good shape.

She tried them on, and to her delight, they fit comfortably. She scanned over the contours of the insoles, moulded by Auntie Lynn's feet over countless adventures. There was another piece of her aunt still with her, guiding her on her journey.

Dressed in comfortable attire and laced up with Auntie Lynn's boots, she made her way to the Post Office. Beth was already there, waiting with a smile. Ru noticed she too wore worn-in walking boots, suggesting she was no stranger to the paths they'd be treading.

The two of them began their walk, and as the scenery of Puckleworth unfolded around them, Beth opened up. She spoke of her early years as a teacher, the challenges she faced, and her love for the children she taught. The initial frostiness between them melted away as they shared stories and laughed at shared experiences.

Beth's initial coldness wasn't personal; perhaps it was a protective mechanism or maybe just a bad day. Whatever the reason, the walk turned out to be the bridge that spanned the gap between them.

"How's the garden restoration going?"

Ru's face lit up at the mention of the garden.

"It's been an incredible journey so far. Daniel and I have been working closely, and the garden has come back to life in ways I hadn't imagined. Each day we're uncovering a little more of its hidden beauty."

Beth nodded, her eyes reflecting genuine interest.

"I remember when Lynn used to host gatherings in that garden. As children, we'd play hide and seek among the flower beds and listen to stories under the old oak tree."

Ru smiled, picturing the memories.

"I've found some relics from the past - old toys, a swing covered with ivy, and even some old letters. It's been a walk down memory lane, and like I'm getting to know my aunt better with each discovery."

"It must be therapeutic." Beth mused. Ru nodded thoughtfully.

"It truly is. With every weed I pull out, I feel like I'm letting go of a bit of my past pain. And with every new flower that blooms, I'm reminded of the possibilities of the future."

Beth looked at Ru with a newfound respect.

"It's admirable what you're doing. And it's lovely to see that garden thrive again. Maybe once it's all done, you could host a gathering, just like old times." Ru's eyes sparkled at the idea.

"And Daniel? Word is you too are getting along well?"

Ru blushed. Beth raised an eyebrow, her teasing smile clear.

"Oh, come now, Ru! The village isn't that big, and word travels fast. It's hard not to notice the two of you working so closely together in the garden. Plus, there's a certain... energy when you're around each other."

Ru's blush deepened, but she met Beth's gaze with a sheepish smile.

"Well, yes, we have grown closer. It started with the garden, of course. But as we spent more time together, we realised we had a lot in common. It's been... unexpected, but also really wonderful."

Beth nodded, her gaze softening.

"Life has a way of surprising us when we least expect it. After all you've been through, you deserve happiness, Ru."

The two continued their journey, the path now filled with shared understanding and camaraderie. The once frosty relationship between them had transformed into one of mutual respect and friendship, proving that Puckleworth was a place of second chances and new beginnings.

They bid each other farewell, and Ru made her way back to the cottage. Whilst getting ready she collected some of Auntie Lynn's old books from the study. She wanted to donate them to Shipman's book section so they could be enjoyed by the next reader. On the shelf she noticed a folder labelled *'For Ruth'* down the spine. Her eyebrows drew together as she hadn't noticed it before. As the folder opened, she discovered plastic document wallets filled with pieces of paper bearing her aunt's handwriting along with a letter.

She held the folder with a reverent touch, Ru pulled out the letter, her hands trembling. The familiar loops and swirls of Auntie Lynn's handwriting were a comforting sight, but the context of the folder's contents filled her with a mix of anticipation and trepidation.

My dearest Ruth,

If you're reading this, it means I've left behind the physical realm of our world. It's strange, penning down my thoughts, knowing that you'll read them when I'm no longer around to hold your hand or share a laugh.

I want you to know something important. My disease, as much as it was a challenge, also became a teacher. It made me reflect on life, love and the importance of cherishing moments. In these pages, you'll find snippets of my thoughts, memories, and dreams. Some might be lucid, others might be disjointed — but each one has a piece of my heart.

I've chosen to share them with you, not to burden you with my struggles, but to offer you a window into my world during those times. To help you understand my journey, and hopefully, find bits of wisdom or comfort from it.
Remember, Ru, life is a tapestry of experiences. Some threads might be dark and tangled, while others shine brightly. But together, they create a beautiful, intricate pattern that is unique to each person.

I love you dearly. And I hope, in some small way, these writings can be a bridge that connects our worlds.

Forever in your heart,

Auntie Lynn.

Ru's vision blurred as tears filled her eyes. Carefully, she leafed through the pages in the folder. There were sketches, little poems, memories jotted down, and a few recipes. It was as if Auntie Lynn were sharing her innermost thoughts, confiding in Ru from beyond.

The weight of the moment settled heavily on her. This was a gift, a last connection to her beloved aunt. She took her time going through it. Each page would be read with love, intending to honour the memories and insights Auntie Lynn had shared.

With a soft sigh, she closed the folder, placing it back on the shelf. She would create a special nook in her room, a place dedicated to going through the writings. For now, she had to get ready for her shift at Shipman's, but her heart was lighter, knowing a part of Auntie Lynn was still with her, guiding and comforting her in the most unexpected of ways.

Chapter Sixteen

The days settled into a predictable pattern. Ru's shifts at Shipman's, while monotonous, offered a certain rhythm and structure to her life. Each morning, she would set up the café, aligning chairs perfectly and setting out baked goods. The familiar hum of the espresso machine became a comforting backdrop to the repetitive tasks that made up her day.

The café, with its well-worn wooden floors and vintage ambiance, saw a mix of patrons. New faces would sometimes appear, travellers passing through Puckleworth or youngsters on a day out. But the ebb and flow of Shipman's customers remained consistent, a routine that Ru found solace in.

Yet, amidst this predictability, there were moments that broke the mundaneness. An elderly couple celebrating their golden anniversary with Shipman's famous carrot cake, or a young writer finding inspiration and penning down a poem on a napkin.

Outside of Shipman's, the garden at Blossom Cottage became her haven. Working alongside Daniel, every patch of earth they nurtured or plant they tended brought them closer. Their shared silences spoke volumes, and the mutual respect they had for nature and each other was palpable.

Ru loved the afternoons when the sun hung low, casting long, golden shadows across the garden. Daniel would sometimes share stories of his travels, of the rare plants he had come across, or the curious gardening techniques he had learned. She would recount tales of her life in the city, drawing laughter from him with anecdotes of urban chaos.

Yet, it wasn't all talk. There were moments of quietude. Sometimes, they would sit by the blooming hydrangeas, with a cup of tea, lost in their own thoughts. In these moments, amidst the scent of roses and the gentle touch of the breeze, Ru sensed an unspoken bond with Daniel. It wasn't just the shared task of reviving the garden but something deeper, a mutual understanding that transcended words.

As days turned into weeks, Ru's life seemed like a tapestry of contrasts. The predictability of Shipman's juxtaposed against the ever-evolving beauty of Blossom Cottage's garden. And at the heart of it all was her burgeoning relationship with Daniel.

Amid the routines and budding relationships, a new pattern emerged for Ru – the weekly walks with Beth and Milly. Beth's initial invite had laid the groundwork, and soon after, Milly had expressed her interest in joining. The trio formed an unlikely but harmonious group, with each bringing their own unique energy and perspective.

Every Saturday, they would meet, their starting point varying from week to week. Sometimes they would venture into the neighbouring woods, listening to the chirping of the early birds and admiring the dew-kissed leaves. Other times, they would walk along the riverbank, the sound of the fast flowing water providing a calming background to their conversations. Milly, with her youthful spirit, would often regale them with tales from Shipman's, the little dramas and moments of unexpected joy. Her vibrant energy was infectious, and she often led the group on impromptu detours, chasing after a pretty butterfly or insisting on a detour to pick wildflowers.

Beth, with her years of experience in Puckleworth, acted as the group's unofficial historian. She would point out old landmarks, share snippets of town lore, and often throw in a personal anecdote that had Ru and Milly in splits.

Ru played the role of the keen observer. She absorbed their stories, the changing scenery, and the warmth of the friendship that was blossoming between the three of them. As the weeks passed, the beauty of the changing seasons became a character in their weekly adventures. The air grew warmer, the days longer and the scent of blooming flowers became a constant companion during their walks.

The trio celebrated these transitions in their own little ways. Beth would often pack a light picnic, with sandwiches, fresh fruit, and sometimes a thermos filled with hot tea or cold lemonade, depending on the weather. They would lie out on a blanket in a scenic spot, and for a few hours, the world outside their circle ceased to exist.

These walks, amidst nature's beauty and the camaraderie of friendship, became therapeutic for Ru. They were a reminder of the healing power of human connection and the ever-present beauty around them. And as the landscapes changed, so did Ru's outlook on life. The bleak days of winter and the challenges they brought seemed more manageable, knowing that spring and the warmth of new beginnings were just around the corner.

Chapter Seventeen

By the time Daniel had arrived, Ru was already in the garden. She sat crossed legged with her faithful notebook by the pond they had uncovered. With the colouring pencils she'd found in the desk drawer and Moss the cat curled up next to her, enjoying the gentle strokes, Ru sketched.

As Daniel approached, he slowed down, taking in the serene picture before him. There was something timeless about it - a woman, her loyal feline and nature. The morning sunlight dappled through the trees, casting a soft golden glow over them. It was moments like these that made him fall in love with gardening all over again, where human touch met nature's beauty.

"Mornin' Ru."

Daniel called out softly, not wanting to disrupt the tranquillity of the moment. Ru looked up, her face breaking into a warm smile.

"Hey, Daniel. Got inspired by the pond. Thought it could use more life."

Daniel came closer, kneeling down beside her to get a closer look at her sketches. The intricate lines and shading showed delicate water lilies, cattails, and even a small fountain feature that would recirculate the pond's water, creating a soothing sound.

"It's beautiful." Daniel commented, genuinely impressed.

"Your vision complements the natural setting perfectly.

We can introduce some local aquatic plants, maybe even

a few fish. With your design, this could become a sanctuary for wildlife and a peaceful retreat for you."

Ru's eyes sparkled with enthusiasm.

"Exactly what I was hoping for! I imagined sitting here in the evenings, watching the sunset and listening to the water. A place to relax and reflect." Moss, sensing the shared excitement, stretched lazily, his tail flicking contentedly.

"Seems like Moss approves, too."

They spent the next hour discussing the feasibility of the project, the materials they'd need, and the plants that would best fit the pond's ecosystem. As they talked, Ru's design took on a tangible form in Daniel's mind.

After lunch, they worked together in a stubborn section of the garden. Amidst the brambles, Ru found a rope. She lent down and pulled on it however, it wouldn't budge. A few more tugs and still it wouldn't move. She continued to pull however, lost her footing and fell into Daniel. He lost his balance and they both rolled over a log and fell to the floor.

For a moment, time seemed to stand still. They were in a tangled heap, with Ru's face inches from his. Both were covered in dirt and bits of leaves, and their surprised expressions mirrored each other's.

Ru's heart raced, not just from the fall, but from the sudden proximity to Daniel. His eyes, usually filled with determination when working, now held a glint of amusement mixed with surprise. She became hyper-aware of every point of contact between them, from her hand pressed against his chest to their legs entwined in an awkward dance.

"Are you okay?" Her cheeks flushed. Daniel let out a small chuckle.

"Yeah, I think so. Though my pride might be a little bruised," he joked. "What about you? Are you hurt?"

Ru shook her head, trying to regain her composure.

"I'm fine. That rope was more stubborn than I expected. Sorry for the unintended tackle."

She shifted, attempting to untangle herself, but Daniel's hands cradled her in place. Their gazes locked, and the playful atmosphere shifted to something deeper, more intense. He cleared his throat and whispered,

"You know, next time you want to get close, you can just ask. No need for dramatics." Ru laughed, the tension breaking.

"Noted."

With a final chuckle, they disentangled from one another, Daniel helping Ru to her feet. As they brushed off the dirt and resumed their work, there was a new, unspoken connection between them – a mix of camaraderie and the hint of something more.

And while the rope remained a mystery for the moment, it had inadvertently brought them closer in ways they hadn't expected. The rustling of the leaves, the distant chirping of birds, and the gentle swish of Ru's broom against the stone pathway created a tranquil ambiance. Every so often, the rhythmic sounds of Daniel's hammer or the creaking of the fence panel being adjusted punctuated the air.

The day's warmth waned as the shadows lengthened, casting intricate patterns on the garden floor. The two worked in companionable silence, each engrossed in their respective tasks. Still, there was an unspoken understanding that every glance exchanged carried meaning. A subtle acknowledgment of their shared efforts, of the bond that was forming between them, reinforced with every smile, every nod.

Ru wiped her brow, stealing a moment to watch Daniel. His focus on fixing the fence was admirable, but there was an effortless grace to his movements, an inherent connection to the world around him. As if sensing her gaze, he looked up, locking eyes with her. A slow smile spread across his face, prompting a matching one from her.

"You know," Daniel began, setting down his tools and walking over to her, "there's a local tradition that after a day's hard work, the workers share a drink, reflecting on the day's achievements. Interested?"

Ru's eyes sparkled with amusement.

"Is that an actual tradition or just a Daniel tradition?"

He laughed, the sound rich and genuine.

"Maybe a bit of both. But I think we've earned it. What do you say?"

She pretended to contemplate, tapping her chin with her finger.

"Well, I suppose one drink won't hurt. Lead the way."

Daniel gestured towards the back porch of her cottage, where a couple of wooden chairs and a small table stood. He disappeared into the house briefly and returned with two bottles of cider that he'd brought with him early that day.

As they sat, sipping the refreshing drink, they recounted their progress, shared stories, and laughed at the day's minor mishaps. The setting sun cast a warm, golden hue, making the moment timeless.

The evening turned to dusk, and as they drained the last of their cider, both felt a sense of gratitude. Not just for the work accomplished, but for the unexpected bond forming between them, nurtured by shared tasks, laughter and silent exchanges in a garden coming back to life.

"So the barn dance on Friday. Would you like to go together?"

Ru paused, leaning on her chair. The sudden invitation caught her off guard, but the warmth in Daniel's eyes was reassuring. The barn dance was part of a yearly fundraising event in Puckleworth, a tradition that everyone looked forward to. It was a time when the community came together, celebrating the beginning of summer with music, laughter, and dancing.

"I've never been to one," she confessed, brushing a stray lock of hair behind her ear. "But I'd love to."

"Great! It's a lot of fun. And don't worry about the dancing part; I promise I'll lead."

"As long as you promise not to let me trip and tackle someone again."

He laughed, the sound resonating through the garden.

"Deal."

Chapter Eighteen

Another day drew to a close and Ru began her evening routine after she'd finished her shift at Shipman's. The gentle crackle from the fireplace provided a melodic backdrop, its warmth enveloping her as the day's exhaustion settled in. The soft, ambient light from the room's corner lamp painted everything with warmth, making the aged pages of her book glow.

Every so often, Ru would mark her place with her finger, lifting her head to gaze into the dancing flames. Thoughts of the day, of Shipman's, of her blossoming garden and of Daniel flitted through her mind. There was a comforting familiarity to these evenings, a soothing routine that anchored her in this new phase of her life.

Moss, sensing her drowsiness, padded into the room. With a gentle mewl, he leapt onto the couch, curling up beside her, putting vibrations adding to the room's tranquillity. With a contented sigh, Ru leaned back into the cushions, allowing herself to be fully immersed in the moment. The world outside faded, replaced by the soft rustling of pages, the flickering of firelight, and the rhythmic breathing of a woman and the cat who had made Blossom Cottage his second home.

She picked up a photo album and studied the images. The album, with its worn leather cover and frayed edges, was a testament to time. Each photograph captured a fleeting moment, preserving it forever. As Ru flipped through the pages, she was taken on a visual journey through Auntie Lynn's life.

She was the life of every gathering. Photos of her at various parties, surrounded by friends, showcased a woman full of vivacity and joy. From black and white images of her younger days, with her hair in victory rolls and the unmistakable fashion of the 50s, to the vibrant colours of the 70s and 80s, Her infectious smile remained a constant.

But it was the next section of the album that truly caught Ru's attention. There she was, a little version of herself, with chubby cheeks and an impish grin. These images were juxtaposed with those of her parents, moments she barely remembered but had now come to life. The image of her father, tall with a mop of curly hair, holding a baby Ru, made her heart clench. And there they were, her mother and father, looking so in love and so full of hope.

She had so few memories of the three of them together. The years had taken a toll, especially with her mother's battles. Ru's fingers traced the outlines of the faces in the photographs, a lump forming in her throat.

Flipping through, summer memories with Auntie Lynn came flooding back: splashes in the garden, lazy picnics under the sun, building castles on the beach. Each image spoke of love, warmth and the sanctuary she had provided.

As she reached the end of the album, a note, penned in familiar handwriting, tumbled out:

Dear Ruth,

Always remember that family is more than just blood. It's about the people who stand by you, who pick you up when you fall, who love you at your worst. I hope these memories bring you joy and remind you of the love that surrounds you, always.

With all my heart,

Auntie Lynn.

Tears welled up in Ru's eyes. She was becoming very fond of finding these notes around the cottage. The weight of her silent sacrifices became clear. The unsaid understanding that she took young Ru in, not just for summer fun, but to provide a respite from a turbulent household. It was an unspoken act of love, shielding her from the harsh realities of her mother's struggles.

Ru clutched the album close, overwhelmed with gratitude and understanding of the depth of her aunt's love. Amidst the joys and challenges of life, this album was a beacon reminding her of love, sacrifice and the ties that bind.

She felt gratitude for these simple moments of serenity amidst her eventful life in Puckleworth. The book gradually slipped from her grasp, landing on her lap, as she succumbed to the pull of sleep, wrapped in the warmth and safety of her new home.

Suddenly, her phone text tone woke her up. She saw four missed calls and two text messages from the same person on the screen. She read *'Mum Mobile'* and was brought back into full consciousness. The last time she had spoken to her mum was at the funeral. Hesitating for a moment, Ru tapped on the text messages.

"Ruth, please call me."

The second one read:

"It's urgent. I really need to speak with you."

Ru's heart raced, a mixture of anxiety and concern. The strained relationship with her mother was rooted in a complex web of emotions, built over the years as her mother's addiction spiralled out of control. The constant mood swings, broken promises, and chaotic atmosphere at home had compelled Ru to distance herself, both for her well-being and her sanity. Yet, the instinct to care and worry about a parent never truly faded.

She took a deep breath and dialled her mother's number. A frail voice answered. Ru switched the phone to speaker mode so she could hear better.

"Ruth? Is that you?"

"Yes, mum, it's me," Ru replied, trying to keep her voice steady. "You called?"

"Oh, Ruth," her mother's voice quavered. "I'm sorry for disturbing you so late. I... I just didn't know who else to turn to."

"What's wrong, mum?" There was a pause before her mother spoke.

"Ruth, I want to get better. This is a nightmare.. I just... I need help." Despite hearing it before, she still hoped for her mum.

"Ok, where are you now? Are you in a safe place?"

"Am I in a safe place?" Her mother's voice turned aggressive. "Do you think I can't look after myself? Do you believe you're superior to me? Spiteful little girl, who do you think you are?!" Her mum screamed down the phone.

Ru paused and breathed deeply. Unfortunately, her mum had been on this cycle for over 15 years. It was always the same. She'd disappear and not make any contact. The only updates she had were from social media posts. There would be pictures and videos of her mum talking to her followers, encouraging them to cease life.

However, her words did not match up to her actions. She'd reach out to her daughter, seemingly to make amends, then change the moment Ru mentioned anything remotely close to her addiction.

"Mum, it's getting late and I need to go."

"You're leaving me again. You don't have time for your mother? Spiteful child you are, do you know how lucky you are to have a mum? That ivory tower of yours is showing, you and that precious cottage. It should have been mine!" With that, her mum hung up the phone.

Ru stared at the screen, burdened by the conversation. Each of these confrontations left a fresh scar on her heart, reopening old wounds. The oscillation between her mother's genuine cry for help and the aggressive lashing out was a painful dance she had become all too familiar with.

She switched off her phone. When she set it on the coffee table, she leaned back into the couch and took in slow, deep breaths to calm her racing heart. The raw emotions—guilt, sadness, anger, hope and despair—washed over her in waves. She closed her eyes and tried to centre herself.

Memories of better times—when her mother was sober, when they laughed together, shared mother-daughter moments, and when Ru was truly cherished—flashed before her eyes. Those times were distant, like another lifetime.

A soft knock at the door startled her from her reverie. She saw Daniel standing at the living room door, concern etched on his face.

"Sorry, I forgot my screwdriver. The door was open so I let myself in but I heard yelling," he began gently, referring to the outburst he had overheard from the kitchen. "Is everything okay?"

Ru's eyes welled up, and she shook her head, her voice barely above a whisper.

"It's my mum. It's always the same cycle. She calls for help, and then, when I try to be there for her, she pushes me away."

Daniel stepped closer, wrapping an arm around her shoulders, offering silent support. Ru leaned into his embrace, seeking comfort during her turmoil.

"It's okay," Daniel spoke softly, "I'm here. You're not alone."

The two stood there for a while, Ru drawing strength from Daniel's presence. Even in the darkest moments; she wasn't alone. He stayed a short while longer to make sure she was ok. He shared how his Uncle also had an alcohol addiction and how it was incredibly hard for his family. After ensuring Ru's well-being, he retrieved the tools and departed.

Ru watched him leave from her window. She had a sense of gratitude for his unexpected but timely presence. The house grew silent again, but it wasn't a pressing silence anymore. It was more contemplative. Ru brewed herself a cup of chamomile tea, hoping its calming properties would help still her racing heart. As she sipped, she thought about Daniel's words and how, despite the pain, many people found the strength to continue pushing forward.

Perhaps it was the hope that one day things would change or the bonds of love, however strained they might be, that still tethered them to their troubled loved ones. Ru realised she wasn't alone in her struggles. And while each journey was unique, there were shared feelings, shared pains, and shared hopes.

The night outside was quiet, with only crickets chirping. Ru finished her tea, took one last look at the garden from her window – the garden that symbolises a fresh start and new beginnings – and headed to bed, hoping for a peaceful night's rest.

Chapter Nineteen

The following morning as the first light painted the sky, Ru took a different route to work. Her walks with Beth and Milly had provided her with a map of the town so she took one of the routes down a lane. About halfway, her eyes caught sight of an overgrown plot of land. Tall grass waved in the breeze, and a few wildflowers peeked through, hinting at the plot's untamed beauty. At the front of the plot, a sign displayed in bold: *"FOR SALE."*

Curiosity piqued, Ru surveyed the land. It was bordered by old stone walls on three sides and had a small brook running at the far end. The land, though untended, held a sense of potential. It was like an unmarked canvas, waiting for an artist's touch.

Ru tilted her head, lost in thought. The plot intrigued her, beckoning to her with possibilities she couldn't yet define. But there was a stirring, a whisper of an idea forming at the back of her mind.

After pulling herself from her contemplation, she took a mental note of the details on the sale sign and continued her journey to Shipman's. Throughout the day, as she served customers and chatted with colleagues, her mind would occasionally drift back to that plot of land. The image of the wildflowers dancing in the breeze and the untapped potential of the space lingered in her thoughts.

Ru paused briefly to absorb the lively atmosphere at Shipman's café. Every visit was like stepping into a living room filled with extended family members. From the warm scent of the pastries wafting from the kitchen to the low hum of chatter, the café was Puckleworth's heartbeat.

Drawn to its infectiously welcoming atmosphere, she visited on her day off. She pulled up a chair by the window, which gave her a clear view of the scenic garden and the villagers going about their morning routines. She sipped from her steaming cup of coffee, savouring the rich aroma. Children chased each other playfully on the sidewalk, their laughter echoing in the mild morning air.

As she was flipping through a local newsletter, a gentle tap on her shoulder caught her attention. Iris, the owner of the notorious black cat, Moss, smiled at her.

"Mind if I join you, dear?" Iris asked, her eyes twinkling behind her spectacles.

"Of course, Iris. Please do." Ru shifted her belongings to make space.

The older woman settled into the chair opposite Ru, placing a pot of tea and a slice of lemon cake on the table.

"Moss sends his regards. He's taken quite a liking to your garden. I hope he isn't causing any trouble." Ru let out a giggle.

"Not at all! He's been brilliant company, especially during the long gardening sessions. Daniel and I quite enjoy his playful antics." Iris' eyes gleamed with a hint of mischief.

"Oh, Daniel, you say? You're spending quite a lot of time together, aren't you two?" Ru blushed.

"We've been working in the garden. It's an extensive project." Iris nodded, sipping her tea,

"I've heard. It's lovely to see Blossom Cottage coming back to life. It's even lovelier seeing new friendships bloom."

Their conversation meandered through various topics - the upcoming village barn dance, knitting projects, and of course, the escapades of Moss. Before long, they were joined by other familiar faces, and the small table became a lively hub of community updates, shared stories, and laughter.

Mrs H arrived with a large leather book with the title Friends Committee branded across its front. She took a seat. The pages of the book seemed to come alive with memories and vibrant colours. Each photograph told a story, capturing moments of joy, camaraderie and the heart of Puckleworth's community spirit. Auntie Lynn was a central figure in many of them, her infectious enthusiasm clear in her poses and the elaborate outfits she donned.

"Your aunt was quite the creative genius," Mrs H remarked with a fond smile, pointing to a photograph where she was decked out in a flapper dress, pearls cascading down her neck and a feathered headband placed just so.

"This was one of my favourites – the Roaring Twenties event. The entire village hall was transformed into a Gatsby ballroom. It was absolutely splendid."

Ru's eyes widened in amazement as they turned the page to the steampunk-themed event. Brass goggles, intricate corsets, and cog-laden accessories dominated the scene. Auntie Lynn, in a masterfully tailored Victorian outfit adorned with mechanical embellishments, stood proudly next to a steam-powered contraption she'd crafted as a centrepiece. Mrs H highlighted the 50s rock and roll theme as a memorable night.

"The jukebox played non-stop, and we danced to the tunes of Elvis and Chuck Berry till our feet hurt."

Ru was enchanted by the legacy her aunt had left behind.

"She was the life of these events. I can see her touch in every little detail." Mrs H nodded.

"Yes, she poured her heart and soul into these fundraisers. It wasn't just about the money raised, but the unity it fostered within the community. People look forward to it every year."

This was the first year they had run an event without her. In her final few years, she had grown increasingly confused with the themes from different eras. The care home decided it would be best for her not to attend this year's barn dance. Little did they know she would pass away before it arrived.

Ru's walk back to the cottage was filled with reflection about her aunt. The crunch of gravel underfoot seemed amplified as she walked, lost in the storm of her thoughts. The countryside, usually a source of solace and calm, seemed today to echo her internal tumult. Trees, normally standing tall and inviting, appeared like silent mourners, their leaves rustling in the wind as if whispering condolences.

Each step took her back through memories—of Auntie Lynn's warm laughter filling rooms, of her wisdom shared over cups of tea, of the unmistakable scent of her garden after a light rain. She had been her anchor in the turbulent seas of life, a guiding star when the nights were darkest.

Then there was her mother, a stark contrast in Ru's memories. Once vibrant and loving, addiction had cast a long shadow over their relationship. Broken promises, shattered trust, and hazy recollections marred the tapestry of their shared past. The deep wounds and unhealed rifts made it challenging for Ru to reconcile her feelings.

She paused by a small bridge overlooking a stream, the gentle babble of water providing a backdrop to her contemplation. She wished she could separate the disease from the person, both with her aunt and her mother. Where Auntie Lynn's illness had cruelly robbed her of memories and coherence, it hadn't taken her love or warmth. Her mother's addiction stole everything Ru admired in her.

A small bird fluttered by, landing on the bridge railing, its cheerful chirping pulling Ru from her reverie. She realised she needed to come to terms with her feelings. The mourning of her aunt and grappling with the complexities of her relationship with her mother were both valid, yet distinct emotional journeys. They deserved their own spaces in her heart.

Ru took a deep breath and made a silent promise to herself. She would continue to honour Auntie Lynn's legacy by embracing life and contributing to the community she had grown to love. As for her mother, Ru vowed to navigate their relationship, seeking support when needed, and protecting her own well-being.

Ru felt an immediate sense of peace as she stepped into the garden. It was as if every plant, every flower, every blade of grass was trying to comfort her, to offer solace.

She brushed her fingers over the tulip petals, marvelling at the delicate texture. The myriad of colours, from vibrant reds to soft pinks and sunny yellows, seemed to dance as the wind whispered through the garden. She took a moment to close her eyes and let the earthy scent envelop her, grounding her and connecting her to the present.

The bees, diligent in their work, flitted from flower to flower, their soft hum adding to the garden's serenade. They seemed to move with purpose, yet with an undeniable grace, reminding Ru of life's delicate balance between duty and joy.

She found a quiet spot by a newly revitalised rose bush, its buds hinting at the promise of blooms to come. When she sat down, she let the environment wash over her. Every emotion, every memory, every pang of grief, and every flicker of hope.

The more time she spent there, the more she was connected to Auntie Lynn. It was as if, in the rustle of the leaves, the chirp of the birds, and the fragrance of the flowers, she could feel her aunt's presence, guiding her, comforting her, and reassuring her.

As the hours passed and the sun dipped below the horizon, Ru had a renewed sense of strength. The garden showing the cycles of life, death and rebirth had provided her with a profound understanding of her own feelings and challenges.

She rose, taking one last look around, feeling a deep sense of gratitude. Each sunset promised a new dawn. With that thought, Ru returned to the cottage, the garden lessons engraved in her heart.

Chapter Twenty

On the night of the barn dance, as Ru rummaged through her vanity, she found an old lipstick that Auntie Lynn had once gifted her—a classic shade of red, reminiscent of the vibrant hues from the vintage photographs in the leather-bound book Mrs H had shown her. The memories of their shared laughter and beauty secrets whispered in her ear as she applied the colour to her lips.

She gave her hair a soft wave, reminiscent of the styles she'd seen in the 40s and 50s-themed pictures. The process was therapeutic, with each curl bringing back more cherished memories shared with her as a young girl. By the time she was done, her hair cascaded down her shoulders in elegant waves, framing her face.

For her outfit, Ru had chosen a mid-length dress with a chequered pattern, its colours echoing the flowers in her garden. With comfortable heels and a dainty necklace, she looked radiant and ready to dance.

This wasn't just another event; it was a night where she'd honour Auntie Lynn's legacy, mingle with the Puckleworth community, and perhaps even take the next step in whatever was blossoming between her and Daniel.

With a light shawl draped around her shoulders, she stepped out into the evening. The sun had just set, painting the sky with hues of lavender and pink. The starlit path to the venue set the mood for a night of music and fun.

As she walked, Ru's heart was light with anticipation. She was ready to immerse herself into the joyous spirit of the barn dance, making memories that would become part of her own legacy.

Upon entering the village hall, Ru was greeted by a whirlwind of activity. Strings of warm yellow lights hung from the rafters, illuminating the hall with a warm glow. Hay bales were used for both decoration and seating in the room. The walls were adorned with wooden panels, evoking the feel of a rustic barn, and coloured pennant banners added a festive touch.

People milled about, sipping on drinks and chatting. The laughter and hum of conversations mixed with the music. Men sported plaid shirts, suspenders and cowboy hats, their boots tapping along to the rhythm of the band. Women wore flared skirts and dresses, some adorned with playful tassels, others with detailed embroidery, and cowboy boots were a popular choice amongst many. Even the little ones were dressed up, with young boys in waistcoats and bandanas and girls in cute pinafore dresses and braided hair.

Near the entrance, children giggled as they donned cowboy hats and bandanas, posing for pictures against the themed backdrop. The props, which included lassos, toy pistols and sunflower bouquets, added a playful element to the photos. To the side, a refreshment stand was set up, offering traditional barn dance delights—bowls of hearty chilli, cornbread, apple pies, and more. The aroma of the cooked food wafted through the air, making Ru's stomach rumble in anticipation.

As she ventured deeper into the hall, Ru was met with a sea of familiar faces. Iris, donning a cowgirl hat, waved her over and introduced her to a group of friends. Mrs H was amid teaching a group of youngsters some basic dance steps, her enthusiasm infectious. Even Moss, the beloved black cat, was sitting on a hay bale with a tiny cowboy bandanna around his neck.

The energy in the room was captivating. People laughed, chatted, and swayed to the tunes of the barn dance band on a raised platform. The fiddle, banjo and guitar created a harmonious blend that beckoned everyone to the dance floor. She was greeted by familiar faces—Milly gave her a quick hug and complimented her on her dress, and Mrs H, her eyes sparkling with mischief as always.

"Look at you, darling! All dolled up and fitting right in!" Mrs H held Ru's hands and gave them a gentle squeeze.

"Thanks to you and everyone else, I've been so welcomed here."

Just beyond her eyeline her eyes met with Daniel's as he entered the room. He walked toward her. His confident stride and the rugged charm of his attire were noticeable. Ru admired how effortlessly he embodied the cowboy spirit, and the sight of him dressed up in such a manner sent a pleasant shiver down her spine. The world faded away as their eyes locked. As he reached her, he removed his hat with a gentlemanly gesture, revealing his auburn hair tousled just right.

"Evening, ma'am." He greeted her with a playful twinkle in his eye.

Ru caught her breath. She had only seen Daniel in gardening attire, so his transformation was breathtaking. The flannel shirt, unbuttoned to reveal a hint of chest hair, added an alluring touch to his rugged look.

"Wow - You're beautiful," he complimented her, his voice sincere. A soft blush painted Ru's cheeks as she met his gaze.

"Thank you." Her voice was tinged with appreciation and a hint of bashfulness. She returned the compliment, her eyes lingering on him.

"And you clean up pretty well yourself."

"Figured I should try for such a special occasion." His gaze held hers as if savouring the moment. Ru smiled, the chemistry between them palpable.

"And who might you be emulating tonight? John Wayne? Clint Eastwood?"

Daniel pretended to consider it for a moment, his lips curving into a playful grin.

"A bit of both, perhaps? Though I think I've got some competition tonight," he gestured toward the other attendees who were also dressed up in their western-themed outfits.

Their banter flowed, as it always did, but tonight there was something different—an underlying tension, a newfound connection that was impossible to ignore. The barn dance had transformed the atmosphere, and their shared glances held promises of unspoken desires. With a charming smile, Daniel extended his hand toward Ru.

"Would you honour me with a dance?"

Ru's heart skipped a beat again.

"I'd be delighted." She placed her hand on his, feeling the warmth and strength of his grip. Together, they made their way to the dance floor, ready to let the music carry them into a world of shared moments and unspoken feelings.

The lively tunes captivated even the hesitant attendees. Feet stomped in unison, hands clapped, and couples swung each other around with contagious laughter. The music had an undeniable magic, turning even the shyest wallflower into a barn dance enthusiast.

Ru watched with fascination as seasoned dancers manoeuvred through intricate steps, their movements in sync with the rhythm. But it wasn't just the experienced dancers who shone that night. The dance floor was an eclectic mix of all ages and skill levels, united by their shared joy and infectious beats of the band.

During a lively jig, Ru found herself partnered with Mr Smithson. To her surprise, the elderly man displayed a sprightliness that belied his age. He twirled her around with gusto, his eyes gleaming with joy.

"Keep up, young lady!" He lead her through the steps with impressive expertise.

Daniel danced with a grace and ease that made it all seem effortless. She watched him dance with Beth and was drawn to his presence. Their paths crossed, and they shared several dances, their chemistry clear in the way they moved together.

In between dances, groups gathered around tables laden with refreshments, sharing stories, and laughter. The air was filled with the aroma of hearty dishes, and the clinking of glasses punctuated the animated conversations.

As midnight approached, Mrs H stepped onto the stage and took the microphone. She thanked the volunteers and suppliers and announced how much money had been raised. The hall erupted into a resounding applause, the palpable excitement and pride filling the room. £1583 reflected the community's dedication, hard work and unity. Mrs H, standing at the front with the rest of the committee, beamed with happiness, her eyes glistening.

"Every year, I'm astounded by the generosity and commitment of this wonderful community," she began, her voice strong and full of emotion. "This amount will help repair the church roof. Thank you."

The Friends Committee was respected and loved for their inclusive efforts at community events. As the applause continued, Daniel leaned over to whisper in Ru's ear.

"Come with me."

As they ventured further away, the sounds from the barn dance faded into a distant hum, replaced by the soothing chirping of crickets and the gentle rustle of leaves. Festoon lights above painted a golden hue around them, their gentle glow creating a cocoon of intimacy. The intensity between them was undeniable - every glance, every touch was charged with an energy that neither could ignore.

"I've loved getting to know you this past month. You're an incredible woman and well…"

Time seemed to slow as their faces inched closer, the world around them fading into a blur. The sounds of the barn dance seemed to quieten to a mere whisper, leaving just the two of them and the electricity that hung thickly in the air.

Their breaths mingled, a warm dance in the space between them, anticipation building. Danniel's thumb caressed her cheek, his eyes searching her for any signs of hesitation. Ru's heartbeat echoed loudly in her ears, a frenzied rhythm matching the rapid pace of her thoughts. Every moment they had shared, every glance exchanged, every touch lingered a moment too long, all culminating in the single, charged instant.

Just before their lips could touch, a loud crash broke the moment. They turned their attention towards the road and saw a red car speeding towards them, knocking down everything in its way. The car was heading directly towards them, so Daniel dived across Ru to move her out of harm's way and they landed backwards over a hay bale.

Metal scraped, tires screeched, and glass shattered, causing the world to slow down. The festive barn dance turned chaotic as screams erupted and people rushed to see what had happened.

Ru's heart raced, her breath caught in her throat. The suddenness of it all, combined with the potential danger they had just escaped, left her shaken. Daniel pushed himself off her, both of them covered in strands of hay. He locked eyes with her, a mix of relief and concern clear in his gaze.

"Are you okay?" He said between breaths, helping Ru to her feet.

"I am, thanks to you." Her voice trembled as she wiped away the tears.

The red car abruptly stopped after crashing into a tree and a crowd gathered. From the damage, it was clear the impact was severe. Many people ran out and hurried to open the driver's side door. Others were on their phones, likely calling for emergency services.

Daniel gripped Ru's hand and scanned her face for injuries. As the driver's side door was forced open, a gasp echoed through the gathered crowd. Ru, upon glimpsing at the driver, felt her heart drop.

"Mum?"

Chapter Twenty One

The harsh fluorescent lighting of the hospital highlighted the scuffs on Ru's elbows. Her hair hung dishevelled around her shoulders as she clutched a polystyrene cup of coffee. Tears fell from her nose, causing her to use the back of her hand to wipe them off. She smiled as the hospital staff passed her in the small corridor.

The police had not long left. They explained that whilst it would need to go to court, her mother would lose her licence and would be fined a heavy amount. She was looking at community service, too.

They also mentioned that the initial tests revealed a dangerously high blood alcohol level, which was, unfortunately, no surprise to Ru. It seemed her mother's addiction had not just been tearing their family apart, but now it was putting others at risk, too.

Daniel had stayed with Ru all night, providing a silent pillar of support. He sat beside her, his own hair a little tousled, his face etched with concern. He'd place a hand on Ru's shoulder, reminding her she wasn't alone. As dawn finally broke, a nurse approached them.

"You can see her now. She's stable, but quite groggy from the medication."

Ru hesitated for a moment, her feelings a whirlwind of anger, relief, sadness and guilt. She took a deep breath, stood up and followed the nurse, with Daniel close behind.

Her mother looked fragile, a stark contrast to the volatile woman from the phone call just days ago. Machines beeped and hummed around her, their rhythmic noises blending into the background. Ru approached, her emotions threatening to bubble over. Her mother's eyes fluttered open, confused, and then filled with recognition and a deep sadness.

"Ruth." Her voice was raspy.

Ru took another deep breath, her voice shaking.

"Mum, why? Why do you keep doing this to yourself? And now, to put others in danger..."

Her mother's eyes filled with tears, her face contorting with regret.

"Ruth, I'm sorry. I wanted to see you... to talk to you. It started out as just one drink to calm my nerves, and then one became two, and then things got out of control."

The weight of years of unresolved feelings, pain, and regret lay between them. Ru took her mother's hand, clasping it.

"We need to get you help, mum. Actual help. This can't go on."

Her mother nodded, her tears flowing now. Daniel watched from a distance, his heart aching for Ru.

"I know. Things need to change."

Daniel returned to the hospital mid morning with a fresh pair of clothes and a toiletry bag. Everything had been that much of a blur that Ru had completely disregarded the fact that she was still wearing last night's barn dance attire. She thanked him and found a toilet to freshen up.

Her eyes met her reflection in the mirror. The traces of antibacterial gel stung her as she removed her makeup. She scraped her hair tightly into a bun and bathed her grazes in the washbasin. The cool water was soothing, a temporary respite from the whirlwind of emotions she felt. Each drop that ran down her hands seemed to cleanse and ground her. The barn dance, the laughter, the shared connection, and then the unexpected accident — all seemed like fragments of a disjointed dream.

Daniel had been her rock throughout, his steady presence a constant source of comfort amidst the chaos. His touch, the way he held her hand as they followed the ambulance, the concern clear in his eyes—it all spoke volumes.

As she changed into the fresh clothes, a soft cotton t-shirt and comfy leggings, she felt a small measure of normalcy return. The hospital's sterile environment, with its harsh lights and the constant hum of machinery, felt alienating. Yet, knowing Daniel was just outside, waiting, provided solace.

Ru stood with her feet firmly planted, pressing her toes into the ground to steady her nerves. This wasn't how she'd imagined the night ending, but life had a way of throwing curveballs. She opened the door and stepped out into the corridor, searching for Daniel.

She found him seated on one of the waiting chairs, his posture tense, fingers drumming anxiously on his knee. He looked up as she approached, relief flooding his features.

"You okay?" he asked, his voice laced with concern. Ru nodded, offering a small smile.

"Much better thanks."

Daniel stood, enveloping her in a gentle embrace, careful not to press too hard against her grazes.

"I'm just glad you're alright."

They took a moment, standing in the corridor, drawing strength from each other. As her mum only suffered minor bumps and bruises, the hospital was eager to discharge her later that day. They got back to the cottage in the early evening. Ru made up a makeshift bed for herself on the sofa and ushered her mum upstairs.

After drawing her a bath, Ru observed her mother, a shadow of the woman she once knew. Gone was the vivacious spirit, replaced by a weariness that seemed to have settled deep within her bones. The cascading water released her mother's long-held tension. She remembered simpler times when she was a child, and her mother would bathe her, their laughter echoing through the house. How had things become so twisted and strained between them?

Ru broke the silence.

"Stay here with me whilst you get yourself back on your feet. Don't worry about what anyone thinks."

"That's very kind, but we both know I can't. I know a place close to here. I'd already enquired there before I came down. They have a spot waiting for me after I found a charity which offers funding. I'm due to check in tomorrow for 6 weeks. It's best if I go away and sort myself out with trained professionals. I never wanted this. It began as a way to cope with your father's passing."

"I was so young, I can hardly remember him."

Her mother's gaze turned distant, filled with a mix of nostalgia and pain.

"He was a good man, Ru. He loved us both. I think I never processed the grief. The burden of raising you alone became overwhelming. Drinking numbs the pain for a little while."

Ru nodded, absorbing her mother's words.

"I always felt his absence, even if I didn't understand it. I wish I had more memories of him. All I have are vague snippets and the stories you used to tell me."

"Once I'm better, once I'm... sober, we can revisit those memories together. I can tell you more about him. About us. Before everything went dark."

Ru squeezed her mother's hand.

"I'd like that. We both deserve to remember the happy times."

A heavy pause followed, the weight of years of unsaid words and pent-up emotions pressing down on them. But beneath that weight was also a burgeoning sense of hope. A chance for redemption, for healing, for rebuilding the shattered bond between mother and daughter. Ru spoke up again.

"This cottage is always open for you when you return from the program. We can work through everything, step by step."

Her mother looked at Ru, eyes shimmering with tears.

"Thank you, my love. I promise I'll do my best. For both of us."

The foundation for a fresh start was set. A beginning filled with understanding, patience and a love that, despite all odds, refused to be extinguished.

Ru returned downstairs to find Daniel making himself busy by fixing a shelf that was wonky. He set the tools down and leaned on a chair. The air was still. She collapsed into his arms. His powerful embrace seemed to wrap around all her broken pieces, holding her together when she was falling apart. They remained intertwined, finding solace amidst chaos.

"I'm here." His voice vibrated against her. "Whatever you need, Ru. I'm here."

Tears flowed. They weren't just tears of sadness or frustration, but also tears of gratitude. She pulled back and looked up into his deep, caring eyes.

"Thank you. I can't express how much your support means to me."

He whisked a tear from her cheek with his thumb. She gave a weak smile, her eyes still red from crying. The room was silent, only their breaths and heartbeats in sync. The recent events had shaken Ru, but in that moment, wrapped in Daniel's embrace, she was grounded and safe.

As night fell, they sat side by side, exchanging soft words and comforting silences. The bond between them grew stronger with each passing moment, built on mutual respect, understanding and a connection that moved beyond words.

Daniel eventually headed to the door and said goodnight to Ru. She hesitated, then lent in to kiss him, but he stopped her and held her face in his hands.

"Not now, not like this."

His words were gentle, carrying a depth of understanding and patience. His touch was comforting, a warm contrast to the cool evening air that filtered through the ajar door. Their eyes locked, both sets filled with a myriad of emotions, from surprise to anticipation to mutual respect. Ru felt a blush creep into her cheeks, her heart racing. She nodded slowly, appreciating his integrity.

"You're right." Her voice was barely audible. "I'm sorry. It's just... everything that's happened. It's been so overwhelming."

"I get it. Emotions run high during times like these. We'll find our moment when the time is right."

She gave a small, appreciative smile.

"Thank you, Daniel, for everything. I don't know how I would've coped without you."

He squeezed her hand.

"You're stronger than you give yourself credit for, Ru. You never have to go through anything alone."

Daniel stepped out into the night, leaving Ru lost in thought. Amidst the chaos, she found strength in him. As she closed the door behind him, she felt a strange mix of exhaustion and hope.

Chapter Twenty Two

The drizzling rain, though light, had formed tiny rivulets that ran across the cobblestones leading to the entrance of the village hall. The festive lights, which once glowed brightly, now lay tangled and partially crushed. Some still flickered sporadically, casting a ghostly shimmer across the wet ground. The chequered tablecloths, which were once symbols of the merry events held here, hung limply on the few outdoor tables that had survived, stained by mud and water.

Even nature seemed to have paused in reverence, as the usually chirping birds remained silent. The splintered tree, an old maple that had stood for generations, was perhaps the most heart-wrenching sight. Its gnarled branches, which had provided shade and solace for countless gatherings, now lay broken, scattered haphazardly around.

Mrs H, her silver hair tightly pulled back, and spectacles perched on her nose, wore her signature navy-blue raincoat. Every wrinkle on her face bore the stories of years spent nurturing the community, and now, those very lines deepened with determination to rebuild. She held a clipboard, which had lists, tasks and instructions covered in a clear plastic sheet to protect it from the rain.

The whiteboard under the gazebo was meticulously divided into sections, each marked with colour-coded post-its. Blue showed areas that needed immediate attention, yellow for tasks that volunteers could handle, and red for those that required professional intervention.

Young Finn, with his bright green wellies, was enthusiastically gathering the small tree branches, his cheeks flushed with both the cold and the thrill of responsibility. Nearby, Mrs Jenkins, a retired carpenter, and Daniel were deep in discussion, rulers and pencils in hand, as they brainstormed a temporary solution for the damaged fence line.

A makeshift first aid station had also been set up, manned by Beth. Thankfully, her services were mostly unneeded, save for a few minor scrapes and cuts during the cleanup.

Mrs H, amidst supervising and organising, took a quiet moment for herself. She gazed at the tree and its surroundings, not just seeing the damage, but visualising its return to glory. The detailed plans in her mind were not just about restoration but also rejuvenation.

Ru approached Mrs H whilst she handed out hot drinks from an urn. She quietly stood next to her and tidied an area of the table.

"Ru, you must be exhausted. How's your mum?"

"She'll survive. I dropped her off at the rehab centre this morning. We've agreed that I would visit in a few weeks once she's settled in. It feels different this time. The crash provided valuable perspective."

"Yes, I can imagine."

Ru looked around, her eyes filling with tears.

"I can't believe this. This is all just too much. Mum, my aunt and now this has brought up feelings about my Dad - how can I grieve someone I didn't even know? If he hadn't been taken from us when I was so young, then maybe mum wouldn't have got to where she is now? Maybe we'd have visited more. We may have had more time together."

Ru sniffled, her face buried in Mrs H's shoulder. She rocked Ru as she would with a child, offering a comforting presence.

"You know, my dear, it's okay to be overwhelmed and feel all these emotions. They make you human. And it's okay to grieve for the what-ifs, for the missed moments, for the lost opportunities. They are a part of your story, and it's important to acknowledge them."

Ru pulled back, wiping her eyes.

"I just wish I could have some clarity, some direction."

Mrs H squeezed her hand, her eyes kind but also piercing with wisdom.

"Life isn't always about having answers. Sometimes, it's about navigating through the uncertainties, learning as you go, and allowing yourself to feel. Grief, pain, joy, love – they're all part of the journey."

Ru dried her eyes.

"Thank you. Your words always seem to offer so much comfort."

"I've been through my fair share of life's difficulties. But through it all, I've learned that every challenge, every heartbreak also brings an opportunity for growth and healing."

As the day wore on, Ru wanted to thank everyone for helping to clear up her mum's mess. She returned from the store with sandwiches, hot drinks and an array of snacks to accompany. She laid out three tables and created one long seating area for all the volunteers.

Whilst she was plating up the food she noticed a framed picture on the wall. Front and centre was her aunt in an apron, serving food. She smiled at the parallels of her efforts. Auntie Lynn would have helped with the cleanup. A warmness flooded over Ru and her heart filled with tangible joy. She closed her eyes and smiled, seeming to have arms wrapped around her.

"You're here aren't you?" she said.

People began gathering around the tables, taking a break from the cleanup efforts. The aroma of freshly brewed tea and coffee filled the air, blending with the scent of the rain-drenched earth.

Ru was at the centre. She distributed sandwiches, poured drinks and made sure everyone was well-fed. The grateful smiles and words of appreciation from the volunteers fuelled her spirits. Despite the weight of the recent events, seeing the community come together and support one another was heartwarming.

As Ru moved among the volunteers, distributing sandwiches and hot drinks, there was a gentle and unspoken understanding among the community members. One by one, they approached her, offering a warm smile and a few words of concern that didn't pry too deeply into her family's situation but expressed genuine care for her well-being.

Beth was the first to step closer. She placed a gentle hand on Ru's shoulder and asked,

"How are you holding up? We've all been thinking about you and your mum. If there's anything you need, you know we're here for you."

Ru's eyes welled with tears, touched by the surrounding kindness. Duncan, her boss at Shipman's, came over next. He held out a thermos filled with hot tea and said,

"Ru, make sure you're taking care of yourself, too. We've got your shifts covered for now. Take the rest of the week off."

Ru accepted the thermos with a grateful nod, her voice choked with emotion.

"I appreciate it. And thank you for all the work you're doing here."

Other volunteers, old and young, took their turns, showing their support and concern in various ways even Finn, still wearing his wellies, gave her a bright smile and a thumbs-up.

Ru felt the warmth of their collective embrace, the unspoken bond that made this community a genuine family.

Their concern for her well-being was palpable, a reminder that in times of hardship, support and unity were the greatest strengths.

The rain continued to fall, but within the circle of friends, the heart of the community remained strong and undaunted.

Chapter Twenty Three

The weight of the week's events bore heavily on Ru's shoulders. Every corner of the village seemed to echo with whispers and unspoken thoughts about the incident. The memories of the barn dance, which should have been filled with laughter and joy, were overshadowed by the screech of tires, broken glass, and the shock that followed.

The kitchen became Ru's sanctuary. Here, amid the familiar hum of the fridge and the comforting scent of freshly baked bread, she tried to find normalcy. As she prepared her morning tea, she found her thoughts drifting back to the fateful night. She pictured her mum, a cocktail of emotions - vulnerability, fear, regret and a desperate need to escape the shackles of addiction.

Ru's heart ached with a myriad of conflicting feelings. Anger at her mother for her reckless actions, fear for what could have happened, and a deep-seated pain for the mother she once knew – the one buried beneath years of battling alcoholism. Yet, there was also a reluctant admiration for the courage her mother had shown by accepting her flaws and checking into rehab. It was a step many in her condition would never take.

She sipped her tea, letting the warmth spread through her, seeking the clarity that seemed just out of reach. The days ahead would be filled with challenges. There would be whispers, sideways glances and a village trying to come to terms with the near-tragedy. But there would also be support, understanding, and a community ready to rally together.

Ru decided. She would be there for her mother, guiding and supporting her through her recovery journey. It wouldn't be easy, and there would be moments filled with doubt and frustration. But if her mother will take the hard path to redemption, Ru would walk alongside her, step by step.

During her reflections, the phone rang. The caller ID showed the name of the rehab centre. She inhaled deeply then answered, ready to face the next chapter on this tumultuous journey.

"Hi mum, how are you?"

"I'm not doing too bad, thanks. The food isn't the best, but I've got a wonderful view from my bedroom."

"That's great mum - are you up for a visitor?"

"Listen love, I've been speaking with the therapist and I think it's a good idea for you to stay away for a while. The withdrawal symptoms are intense and well, I can't guarantee my emotions in those moments. Please don't see it as me pushing you away. It's out of protection for you. I've done such a poor job of protecting you in the past."

Ru felt a lump form in her throat. The simultaneous feelings of rejection and relief were palpable. A part of her was eager to see her mother, to offer comfort and be a pillar of support during this transformative journey. Another part, however, understood the rationale behind her mother's words. She took a moment, inhaling deeply to steady herself before replying.

"Mum, I... I understand. I just want you to get better, and if staying away for a while helps, then that's what I'll do. Can I write to you at least?"

There was a pause on the other end, the silence thick with unsaid words and emotions.

"Thank you and yes please do. It means a lot to me you're understanding. I just... I need to confront and deal with these demons head-on, with no distractions. It's been years of hiding and running, and now's the time to face them."

Ru's eyes welled with tears.

"I'm proud of you, mum. This is difficult, I know. But remember, whenever you're ready, I'll be right here waiting." Her mother's voice cracked.

"I love you, Ruth. I hope one day I can make up for everything."

The weight of those words hung in the air long after the call ended. Ru stared at the phone, processing the conversation. This was just the beginning of a long and arduous journey, one paved with challenges, self-discovery, and healing. But there was hope, a glimmer of light amidst the darkness. And for now, that was enough.

Chapter Twenty Four

The rhythmic hum of bluetits filled the warm, midday air as Ru continued her solitary work in the garden. The persistent sun beat down on her back, casting a dappled pattern of shadows from the branches of the tall oak tree nearby.

Her hands moved with a sense of purpose as she carefully painted the garden fences with a warm cream colour. Each stroke of the brush brought the wood to life, contrasting beautifully with the vibrant explosion of flowers that surrounded her. The recent spell of rain had worked its magic, coaxing the blossoms to burst forth in a riot of colours, as if they were celebrating their newfound life.

The melody of lamb bleats echoed across the evergreen hills, their playful bounces and curious antics providing delightful entertainment during Ru's well-deserved breaks. She would watch the young lambs as they frolicked in the fields, their energy and innocence serving as a reminder of the renewal and growth happening all around her.

As the sun began its descent, casting a warm, golden glow over the garden, Ru stepped back to admire her work. The cream-coloured fences now framed the vibrant flowers, providing a sense of unity and order to the once-wild garden. The sense of accomplishment filled her with a profound satisfaction.

The solitude of these days had given her time to connect with her thoughts, memories and the land. It was a reminder that beauty could emerge from even the most neglected places. With the garden's makeover almost finished, Ru felt a sense of contentment. As the birds continued their song, she knew that the work she was doing wasn't just about making the cottage her own; it was about honouring Auntie Lynn's memory and creating a place of beauty and growth, both in her life and in the garden that she loved.

After having a bath, she threw on some loungewear and made her way into the study. She curled up on the armchair which had been moved from the living room and pulled out a gardening book on growing vegetables. The sips of chamomile tea soothed her mind and she nestled in for an evening of study.

At sunset, she peered over the book and noticed a glow of light coming from the garden. Curiously, she set the book down and looked out of the window. Her eyebrows pulled together as she opened it and heard music.

She grabbed her cardigan and made her way downstairs and out into the garden to find Daniel. Surrounded by a string of festoons, he stood next to the vinyl record player that was playing the day they met. The soft lighting created a scene of dreamlike quality. Each bulb gleamed like a firefly, painting the patio and the surrounding blooms in a warm and intimate glow. The very air seemed charged with an ethereal electricity.

Daniel, under the soft lighting, looked different. Not the gardener or the friend she'd been getting to know, but a man, earnest in his intent, asking for a dance without words. The smooth, timeless notes of Etta James' 'At Last' flowed effortlessly into the night, wrapping around them, and sealing this moment in time. He grinned playfully, acknowledging this was now their song.

Ru's heart raced as she took a hesitant step forward, the evening's surprise sentiment rendering her momentarily speechless. She blinked and emotions welled up. As she approached, the soft strains of the music became clearer, and the sight before her came into sharper focus. She glanced down at Daniel's outstretched hand, noticing the faint tremble.

"Why?" she said, the emotion clear in her voice, not entirely sure if she was asking about the setup or the timing. Daniel's eyes met hers, and for a moment, they shared an unspoken understanding.

"Sometimes, life needs moments like these. Moments that remind us of the beauty in the unexpected. And sometimes, we just need to dance."

His voice was gentle, the underlying emotions raw and clear. Ru's eyes searched his, trying to comprehend the depth of this gesture. She slowly extended her hand, placing it in his, allowing the warmth and steadiness of his grasp to anchor her.

"I'm sorry I've not been around the past few days. I wanted to give you some time."

Ru looked up into his eyes, finding understanding and patience within them. The soft evening glow of the lights bathed the patio. The gentle hum of evening birds and the distant sound of the town blended harmoniously with the soft music playing from the speaker nearby.

"It's okay." her voice choked with emotion. "I think I needed that time, too. To process and come to terms with everything."

He pulled her closer, his hand warm and reassuring against her back.

"I wanted to be there for you, but I also didn't want to overwhelm you. I know how complex feelings can be in situations like this."

Ru nestled her head against his chest, taking solace in the steady rhythm of his heartbeat.

"You being here now, understanding with no need for explanations, means more than you can imagine."

The twinkling lights, the scent of blooming flowers, the rich undertones of the music, all converged, creating a cocoon around them. Their movements were hesitant at first, slowly falling into rhythm with the song.

When the song ended, they stood still, caught in the moment's spell. Daniel looked down at Ru, his eyes reflecting the softness of the evening. The world around them seemed to hush, as if holding its breath. The distance between them grew smaller, the charged space filled with anticipation. Both were very much aware of the beating of their own hearts, each thump echoing the tempo of the song that had just played.

Ru looked up, her eyes glistening with emotions that shimmered like starlight, her gaze locked with Daniel's deep green ones. The air between them thickened with a raw, palpable tension.

With a gentle pull, their faces drew closer, and as their lips met, a cascade of emotions flooded them. The kiss was soft, hesitant at first, like the whisper of the wind rustling through the leaves. But as moments passed, it deepened, becoming more intense, more passionate, echoing the pent-up feelings that had been building.

The garden, with its twinkling lights and soft melodies, blurred into insignificance. All that mattered was the feeling of connection, the warmth of the moment, and the realisation that something profound had shifted.

When they finally pulled apart, they were both left breathless, eyes wide and cheeks flushed. The surrounding night seemed to shimmer with newfound magic and welcomed the turn their relationship had just taken.

Neither of them spoke immediately, words seeming superfluous. Instead, they stood there, hands still entwined, basking in the afterglow of their shared moment, letting the silence speak for itself.

Chapter Twenty Five

The next morning was quiet, save for the distant chirping of birds. A light that streamed in was gentle, bathing the room in a warm glow, emphasising the contours and lines of Daniel's back.

Ru lay there for a moment, taking in the scene's intimacy. The weight of the previous night's events, the dance, the kiss, all culminated into this serene moment. It felt like they were in a tranquil bubble, protected from the rest of the world. The reality of their shared night hung in the air, wrapped around them like a comforting blanket.

She lifted her hand, letting her fingers dance lightly on Daniel's back. They moved in slow, lazy patterns, each touch an exploration, a silent acknowledgment of their deepening connection. She felt the rhythm of his steady breathing beneath her fingertips, and she could almost hear the beating of his heart.

Daniel stirred, the sensation of Ru's gentle touch pulling him from the realms of sleep. He turned to face her, his eyes still hazy with remnants of dreams. They locked eyes, and in that shared gaze, words weren't needed. The depth of their connection, the understanding, the budding feelings, all were communicated in that silent exchange.

"Good morning," he said, his voice rough with sleep. Ru smiled, her eyes reflecting the warmth she felt.

"Morning."

For a while, they lay there, simply enjoying the closeness, letting the morning unfold naturally around them. The world outside could wait. For now, all that mattered was the two of them, and the new chapter they were beginning together.

Ru set up breakfast outside on the patio, the mild morning offering a promise of longer days in the season. She admired the festoons Daniel had hung last night. With her feet curled beneath her, she twirled her hair around her fingers, reminiscing of the night she'd just spent with Daniel.

The sun was just beginning its ascent, casting the garden in a soft, golden light. Delicate chirping of birds provided a gentle soundtrack to her musings. Everything seemed more vibrant, more alive. Even the flowers in the garden seemed to bloom brighter, their petals opening up to the world as if echoing her own awakening.

Memories of the night before played like a cherished film reel in her mind. The way Daniel's eyes had searched hers, the lingering touches, the whispered words. Many vulnerabilities were shared and barriers let down. Every shared laugh, every stolen glance—it had all led to that one magical night.

She thought of the way their conversations had flowed effortlessly, the deep, meaningful topics they had delved into, their dreams, fears and aspirations. And then the transition from words to actions, from verbal intimacy to a physical connection.

A gentle breeze brought with it the scent of blooming roses from the garden. The fragrance seemed to encapsulate the essence of the moment—sweet, intoxicating, and fleeting. A soft meow from Moss brought Ru back to the present. She smiled down at the cat, who seemed content to bask in the morning's warm sun, occasionally glancing up at her with those knowing feline eyes.

There was a newfound sense of contentment within her, a peace she hadn't felt in a long time. The uncertainties of the future still lingered, but for now, everything felt right in the world. Daniel emerged from the cottage, his steps light as he leaned in and kissed her softly.

"Well, what do we have here?" he pressed his lip against hers, his voice still husky from sleep. Ru smiled, her eyes still closed as she savoured the moment.

"Just a little treat." She pulled away to look up at him. There was a warmth in his eyes, a tenderness that mirrored her own feelings.

He took a seat opposite her, reaching for a piece of toast, but not before giving her another lingering look.

"I think Moss missed me." Right on queue the feline leaped onto his lap, purring loudly.

"Or maybe he's just hungry." Ru teased, passing him the jar of jam. They both laughed, the sound echoing in the still morning air. Their breakfast was a simple affair, but every bite, every sip of coffee was infused with the joy of shared intimacy. As they ate, they chatted about the day ahead, the garden plans, and their hopes for the summer. But underlying their casual conversation was a deeper understanding, a shared bond that had been strengthened by the events of the previous night.

The sun continued its ascent, bathing the patio in its golden glow. Time stood still. Nothing else mattered but the two of them and the life they were building together. As breakfast drew to a close, Daniel reached across the table, capturing Ru's hand in his.

"Thank you." His thumb caressing her knuckles. "For last night, for this morning, for everything."
Ru squeezed his hand, her heart full.

"Thank you for being here."

Later that day, Ru began her shift at Shipman's. She removed the clean cups from the washer and stacked them neatly on the reclaimed scaffolding board shelf. The café was busy this afternoon and things settled back down to normal. Milly came bouncing behind the counter to greet Ru. She'd just started her shift as well and was fixing her hair in the coffee machine reflection.

She greeted Ru and could instantly tell something was different about her. She directed her curiosity into a barrage of questions. Ru chuckled, adjusting her apron.

"Am I that easy to read?"

Milly winked, tying her hair into a messy bun.

"Oh, come on. I can tell when there's a certain... glow about you."

Ru felt her cheeks heat.

"I had an... interesting night," she hedged, her thoughts drifting back to the dance with Daniel. Milly leaned in, her eyes gleaming with mischief.

"Did it have anything to do with a certain garden centre owner?"

Ru playfully swatted at Milly, but her smile gave her away.

"Alright, alright, maybe a little."

Milly let out a triumphant laugh.

"I knew it! There's a certain light in your eyes. You two are absolutely adorable together."

Ru shook her head, trying to deflect the teasing.

"Enough about that. We've got a café full of customers to tend to."

"Later, you're spilling all the details."

Throughout their shift, the two women worked in harmony, pouring drinks, serving pastries, and sharing light-hearted banter. The weight of the past week seemed to lift. The familiar rhythm of Shipman's, with its bustling activity and friendly chatter, offered a refuge for Ru, a reminder that life goes on, bringing with it both challenges and moments of pure joy. The café emptied, leaving just a few regulars enjoying their afternoon coffee. Milly leaned against the counter, shooting Ru a knowing look.

"Alright, Miss Mysterious. Spill the beans." Ru laughed, her heart light.

"Okay, okay. Dancing, some deep conversations, and... well, let's just say it feels like a new beginning."

Milly's grin widened.

"That's what I wanted to hear! Life's too short not to cherish these beautiful moments." Ru nodded, a contented sigh escaping her lips.

"You're right. Amidst all the chaos and heartbreak, these brief moments of happiness truly matter."

Chapter Twenty Six

After several days off from the garden at Blossom Cottage, Daniel and Ru were back to work. Every morning began with shared plans over breakfast, discussing the areas that needed attention and envisioning the potential for each space. The garden, once a reflection of neglect, had become a canvas on which they painted their shared dreams.

The roses were pruned to perfection, their thorns now guarded by Ru's delicate gloves, which Daniel had gifted her, jokingly citing her "tendency to take on the more prickly challenges." The vegetable patch was meticulously planned, with Ru's knowledge from her evening readings and Daniel's practical experience guiding their choices. Tomatoes, bell peppers, cucumbers and herbs sprouted, promising a bounty in the seasons to come.

The synergy between them was palpable. Where Ru was meticulous and detailed, Daniel brought strength and vision. They complemented each other seamlessly, their efforts merging to create a garden that was both functional and aesthetically pleasing. But more than the work, it was the moments in between that stood out.

Each touch, each shared look, and even the silence between them was charged with a newfound intimacy. They had grown closer, not just as two people restoring a garden, but as two souls connecting on a profound level.

As they worked side by side, their hands occasionally brushed against each other, sending sparks of electricity. The mundane act of planting flowers or moving a rock became an intimate dance, a chance to communicate without words. Ru would sometimes find Daniel staring at her with a softness in his eyes, and she would blush, her heart racing.

The garden, with its blossoms and scents, became a canvas upon which they painted their growing affection. The roses seemed redder, the lilies more fragrant, and the chirping of birds seemed like a melody celebrating their connection.

During their breaks, they would sit close, sharing stories of their past, dreams of their future, and everything in between. Sometimes, they would simply lie on the grass, looking at the clouds, their fingers entwined, feeling the pulse of the earth beneath them and the rhythm of their heartbeats in sync.

By the end of the week, the once-neglected space had transformed into a beautiful oasis, every nook and corner resonating with the love and care they had poured into it. The garden was alive with vibrant colours, melodious bird songs and the fresh scent of blooming flowers.

They stood at the garden's entrance, hand in hand, admiring their handiwork. The setting sun painted the sky in shades of pink and orange, casting a warm glow over everything.

"We did it!" Her voice filled with pride and emotion. Daniel squeezed her hand, his gaze never leaving the garden.

"We did…together."

They went out for dinner to celebrate finishing the garden. Ru was excited, not only about food but also about getting dressed up and stepping out with Daniel by her side in their first debut.

As she rifled through her wardrobe, she decided on a simple yet elegant navy blue dress that belonged to her aunt. It was vintage but in pristine condition, paired with simple teardrop earrings and matching heels, her outfit fitted her perfectly. Daniel arrived, looking dapper in a crisp white shirt and charcoal trousers. The moment he saw her, his eyes widened and a genuine smile graced his lips.

"You look stunning." He murmured as he helped with the clasp of her necklace, planting a kiss on her neck. The energy, once again, charged with electrical desire.

"We're never going to make it to dinner if you keep kissing me like that." Her own lips pressing against his. Daniel smirked, his blue eyes twinkling mischievously.

"Well, maybe dinner can wait a bit," he teased, pulling her closer. The distance between them disappeared as their lips met once again, more fervently this time.

The room, with its dim lighting seemed to condone their intimacy, wrapping them in a cocoon of warmth and affection. Every touch, every sigh further deepened their connection. They were two souls intertwined, celebrating not just the present moment, but the potential of what lay ahead.

They pulled apart, their breaths mingling. Ru's eyes sparkled with mischief.

"As much as I enjoy this, I'm starving." She traced her fingers along the line of his jaw. Daniel brushed a stray strand of hair behind her ear.

"Alright, alright, dinner it is. But dessert..." he leant in close, "might just be back here."

The path to The Crown And Thorns was paved with cobblestones, and with the sun setting on the horizon, the golden hues painted everything in an ethereal light. Houses along Willow Lane had ivy crawling up their stone facades, and the gentle breeze carried with it the soft fragrance of blooming wisteria.

Every so often, laughter or the faint notes of a song would drift from the open windows of the homes they passed, painting a picture of cosy family dinners. As they walked, Ru glanced up at Daniel, her eyes reflecting the calm contentment she felt.

"It's strange," she mused, "how I've been here for a while now and haven't visited the local pub. Auntie Lynn used to rave about their fish and chips."

Daniel tightening his arm around her waist.

"You're in for a treat. The Crown And Thorns is more than just a pub. It's an institution here. People come for the food and stay for the stories and the company."

When they arrived at the pub, the soft hum of conversation greeted them. Its dark wooden beams and low ceilings created an ambiance of warmth and familiarity. Walls adorned with old photographs and knick-knacks spoke of the pub's rich history and the many generations it had catered to. A friendly barmaid with rosy cheeks and a beaming smile greeted them.

"Ruth? Is that you? I remember you visiting with Lynn when you were younger! How've you been?"

Ru smiled, taken aback by the recognition.

"I've been well, thank you. It feels good to be back. And this is Daniel." The barmaid nodded with a knowing smile.

"Yes, we all know Daniel. It's good to see you."

They found a cosy nook by the window, and as the evening progressed, the pub filled with the soft clinks of glasses, hearty laughter and the rich aroma of classic British dishes. They indulged in the acclaimed fish and chips, along with shepherd's pie and a local ale.

Throughout dinner, they exchanged stories, spoke of their dreams, and often found themselves lost in shared laughter or moments of comfortable silence. The atmosphere of the pub, with its rich history and friendly faces, seemed to weave its magic around them, drawing them closer than ever.

As Ru and Daniel sat at their corner table, they noticed their friends. The half of the Friends Committee that was in attendance had taken a table nearby, their smiles and knowing glances not going unnoticed. Their close-knit group had been privy to the evolution of Ru and Daniel's relationship from the beginning. From the moment they'd met to the spark that had ignited at the barn dance, their friends had seen the connection deepen and blossom.

Throughout the dinner, the committee members exchanged meaningful looks and raised their glasses in silent toasts. They knew that the evening marked a significant step in Ru and Daniel's journey. While the pair had been friends first, their love story was one that had unfolded in the most heartfelt way.

By the time they stepped out, the stars had taken their places in the night sky, and the soft glow of the lampposts illuminated their path back. As they made their way up Willow Lane, arms wrapped around each other, the promise of many more shared evenings and cherished memories lay ahead of them. The little town of Puckleworth, with its charm and warmth, had become more than just a place for Ru—it was becoming home.

"I've been thinking of how I can contribute to the community here. Maybe we don't have to wait for the annual fundraiser to fund projects. I've found a small piece of land for sale that I walk past on my way to Shipman's most days. There's still money left over from what my aunt left me and I want to use it to create a community project. We could create a memorial garden for her where we grow fruit and vegetables and teach people how to garden. It will be a place for reflection, lessons and healing."

Daniel looked over at Ru, his eyes reflecting the admiration he felt for her idea. They had paused under a lamppost, its soft light casting a gentle glow around them.

"That sounds incredible, Ru. To use the land as a tribute to Lynn and benefiting the community. It's both touching and impactful."

Ru smiled, her determination shining through.

"I think she would have loved the idea. A space where nature thrives and people come together. But I'll need help, especially in getting the word out and gathering support."

Daniel nodded enthusiastically.

"You have my full support. And I believe everyone would happily rally behind such a cause. This town thrives on community spirit, and a project like this would be close to many hearts."

"I envision raised beds for different vegetables, a serene pond with benches around for reflection, fruit trees dotting the landscape, and perhaps even a small gazebo where gardening classes can be held. It would be a living testament to Auntie Lynn's love for gardening and her belief in community."

"The educational aspect is brilliant," Daniel added, his voice filled with excitement. "Teaching kids and even adults the nuances of gardening, the importance of sustainable living. It's something that will benefit generations."

Ru nodded, her heart filled with hope and determination.

"Yes, and every harvest season, we can organise a community day where everyone can come, help with the harvest, and take home fresh produce. Maybe even set up a small farmer's market. Any proceeds could go back into maintaining the garden and funding other community projects."

"That's the spirit," Daniel said, his tone filled with admiration. "Turning grief into growth, transforming a personal loss into a community's gain. This is what she would have wanted, and I believe, with our combined efforts this dream will come to life."

They continued their walk, discussing further details and plans for the project. By the time they reached her doorstep, the blueprint for 'Auntie Lynn's Memorial Garden' was taking shape in their minds. The seeds of an idea had been sown, and with dedication and love, it promised to blossom into a legacy.

Chapter Twenty Seven

Ru sat on the patio furniture admiring her garden. Her labour of love was finally complete. It had taken a while longer than she thought, but she was now comfortably settled into her new home.

A soft breeze rustled through the foliage, carrying the sweet scent of blossoms towards her. Every corner of the garden told a story, each plant and flower a testament to days of effort, learning, and moments shared with Daniel.

To her left stood the rose bed, with varieties in deep reds, delicate pinks and pristine whites. They were Auntie Lynn's favourites, and they bloomed with a vigour that seemed to echo her enduring spirit. Further down, the vegetable patch thrived. Tomatoes ripened to a vibrant red, cucumbers grew plump, and herbs like basil, rosemary, and thyme spread their aromatic presence.

The old oak tree under which she used to sit had been given a new lease of life. Its base was now surrounded by a ring of bright wildflowers, while a comfortable hammock was strung between its sturdy branches, inviting one to relax and reflect.

Bird feeders hung from various spots, their chirpy visitors adding music to the serene backdrop. The sound of water trickling from a newly installed fountain added to the garden's tranquillity. Ru had specially chosen it for its soft melody, which she found calming during her moments of reflection.

As she sipped on her herbal tea, Ru let her gaze drift to the garden arch at the entrance, covered in climbing jasmine and wisteria. Its purple and white blossoms intertwined, symbolising the merging of memories with present moments.

Her thoughts drifted to the journey she'd embarked on since arriving in Puckleworth. From feeling like a stranger to laying down roots both in her garden and within the community, it had been a transformative experience. And alongside her through it all had been Daniel. Their bond had grown alongside the garden, flourishing with each shared dream and challenge. She checked her watch and then made her way to the real estate offices to discuss her purchase of the plot of land near to Shipman's. With her hair swept up in a bun and her blouse freshly pressed she swung open the office door and was greeted by Sophie Lang.

Sophie, with her chic bob and impeccably tailored suit, exuded an air of professionalism. Her reputation as the best real estate agent in the county was well-known, and Ru felt a mix of anticipation and excitement.

"Ruth!" Sophie exclaimed with genuine warmth, rising from her plush leather chair. "Lovely to put a face to a name. Please, have a seat."

Ru settled into a chair across from Sophie's desk, taking in the organised chaos of paperwork, land maps and property brochures. The soft hum of the air conditioner and the muted chatter from outside Sophie's office provided a comfortable backdrop.

"I'm glad you came by," Sophie began, clasping her hands on the table. "I've had a closer look at the plot you're interested in, near Shipman's. It's a gem."
Ru nodded, her fingers fidgeting with the clasp of her purse.

"Yes, I've been eyeing it for a while. The location is perfect, and I have so many ideas for what to do with the space."

Sophie leaned forward, her eyes bright with interest.

"Do share. I always love hearing about clients' visions."

Ru began outlining her plans. From creating a community garden space to building a small artisan market for local vendors, her ideas flowed seamlessly, painting a vivid picture of a vibrant hub for residents.

Sophie listened intently, nodding in agreement.

"I love it," she finally said, her voice filled with admiration. "You have such a clear vision. This will be a wonderful addition to the community."

Ru smiled, feeling a weight lift off her shoulders.

"Thank you. Now, let's talk about logistics. I'm ready to take the next step."

Over the next hour, they dived into the intricacies of the purchase—paperwork, pricing, and timelines. It was a whirlwind of information, but Ru felt confident with Sophie guiding her. As they wrapped up, Sophie extended her hand across the table.

"Congratulations, Ru. This is the beginning of something beautiful to honour your aunt and help the community."

Ru shook it firmly, her heart swelling with gratitude and excitement. "Thank you, Sophie. I can't wait to bring this dream to life."

As she stepped out of the real estate agents, she bumped into Mrs H. She curiously looked up at the building's sign and then gasped.

"Oh, you're not selling the cottage are you?" She grasped her bag close to her chest.

"No, not at all! Do you have some time? I'd love to take you out for lunch and run something by you."

Ru and Mrs H sat down on a small table in the centre of the room in The Crown And Thorn. Mrs H, with her ever-present curiosity, listened intently. As Ru outlined her plans for the plot of land — the community garden, the artisan market, spaces for local events — Mrs H's eyes widened with each revelation.

"Oh, my dear," she exclaimed, taking a moment to sip her tea, "this is absolutely wonderful! Puckleworth's needed something like this for a while. A place where the community can come together, share, and create. It's simply brilliant!"
Ru smiled, her heart warmed by Mrs H's enthusiasm.

"Thank you. I truly believe that it can become a cornerstone of our community. Auntie Lynn was so involved with the Friends Committee. I wanted to honour her by getting the group involved somehow, perhaps guiding some initiatives, maybe organising events?"

Mrs H tapped her fingers thoughtfully on the table.

"Well, the committee has been looking for ways to become more active in community development. This might just be the perfect opportunity. We have connections, resources and a passion for this town."

Ru nodded eagerly.

"Exactly! And with the committee's involvement, we can ensure that every aspect of the project reflects the needs and desires of the residents."

The two continued discussing potential collaborations, from fundraisers to launch events. Mrs H even mentioned the potential of some retired teachers on the committee who could host workshops for kids in the community garden. As their plates were cleared away, Mrs H leaned in with a glint in her eye.

"Ru, this is a game-changer. Not just for the town, but for the committee too. Your Aunt would be so proud."
Ru reached across the table, giving Mrs H's hand a grateful squeeze. The seeds of a powerful partnership were sown that afternoon, one that held the promise of transforming Puckleworth into an even tighter-knit, thriving community.

Chapter Twenty Eight

The days had grown longer, and the warmth of spring was transitioning into early summer. Puckleworth was bathed in a gentle glow as nature embraced its yearly rejuvenation. Evenings at The Crown And Thorn had transformed; the usually bustling indoor atmosphere had spilled outdoors.

The pub had recently installed a new yurt in its garden, a spacious canvas structure with ornate decorations and soft, ambient lighting. Its design was a blend of traditional and modern aesthetics, creating an inviting atmosphere for patrons eager to enjoy the balmy evenings.

Ru had met Milly and Beth at the pub on a Friday evening, the perfect way to unwind after a long week. When Ru suggested they meet at the pub, Milly had immediately texted back, *"Let's try the yurt!"*, her excitement was palpable even through the message.

And so, the trio found themselves seated at a rustic wooden table within the yurt. The canvas walls rustled in the evening breeze, and the subtle scent of the surrounding flowers permeated the space.

"It's so lovely out here. I can't believe we can finally enjoy the outdoors without bundling up in layers!" Milly said.

"Yes, it's a pleasant change. This yurt adds such a charm to the place." said Beth. Ru nodded in agreement, sipping her cider.

"It's a beautiful addition. Perfect for these warmer months. Can you imagine the stories this place will witness?" Once settled with a glass of the pub's signature cider, Ru took a deep breath.

"So, I've got some news," she began, her eyes sparkling with a mix of excitement and nervousness.
Both Milly and Beth leaned in, curiosity clear on their faces.

"Go on," Milly prodded, her youthful enthusiasm infectious. Ru took a moment, gathering her thoughts.

"Do you remember that plot of land on Carter's Lane I mentioned a while back? The one that's been for sale?"

"Yes, the one you seemed oddly captivated by?" said Beth.

"Exactly. Well, I've decided... I'm buying it." A momentary silence fell over the table before Milly burst out.

"Ru, that's fantastic! What are you planning to do with it?"

"I'm turning it into a community memorial garden for Auntie Lynn." Beth reached out, placing her hand on Ru's.

"That's wonderful news. Please know that you have our full support. If you ever need help, you know where to find us." Milly's eyes twinkled.

"Absolutely! We're with you every step of the way." Ru's heart swelled with gratitude.

"Thank you, both of you. I might take you up on that offer for help!"

The evening continued in high spirits, with the trio discussing potential ideas for the plot, sharing dreams, and toasting to new beginnings. As the evening unfolded, the yurt drew more patrons, each looking to bask in its unique ambiance. A few tables away, a group had started an impromptu game of charades which quickly caught the attention of many, including Ru, Milly and Beth.

One rather enthusiastic gentleman took the lead, much to everyone's delight. With his exaggerated gestures and intense facial expressions, he had everyone in splits. At one point, he attempted to portray a 'graceful swan', which turned into a mix of wobbly leg movements and flapping arms, looking more like a confused chicken.

 Beth, wiping tears of laughter from her eyes, remarked. "That's a swan I'd pay to see again!" Ru leaned in.
"I bet you a fiver he's going to trip over his shoelaces."
"You're on!"

 Sure enough, as he continued his spirited charade, he entangled himself in his own enthusiasm, tripping over his shoelaces and landing, albeit gracefully, onto a nearby bean bag. The yurt erupted in laughter, and the gentleman took a mock bow, furthering the merriment.

 Soon, other patrons joined in the game, each turn more hilarious than the last. When Beth took the stage to depict 'The Leaning Tower of Pisa', she struck a pose leaning too far to her left and almost knocked over their table full of drinks. Milly's quick reflexes saved the day, but not before Ru's cider had drenched the unsuspecting schnauzer that had been snoozing beneath.

 The infectious energy of the yurt had everyone sharing stories, playing games, and roaring with laughter. By the end of the evening, Ru, Milly and Beth had not only enjoyed each other's company but had also formed light-hearted connections with others.

 The trio walked under the starry night and recounted the evening's comedic highlights. Their laughter echoing through the quiet streets showed the joy of shared moments and the magic of unexpected adventures.

Chapter Twenty Nine

Ru decided it was time to open up the garden to the friends she had made since moving to the community. Doubled up to welcome the Summer Solstice, she hired tables and linens from the parish hall and made a makeshift dining area.

The garden itself, which had been lovingly tended to over the past month, was in full bloom, creating a natural tapestry of colours, scents and textures. The once-overgrown space now radiated life and charm.

Daniel, ever the helpful hand, set up a small wooden dance floor on one side, close to where her aunt's vinyl player played jazz tunes. The mellow notes from the records, coupled with the chirping of the evening birds, set a melodious backdrop for the gathering.

The centrepiece of the setup was the long, rustic wooden table covered in crisp white linens. Atop it sat an array of vases filled with fresh flowers from Ru's garden, creating a vibrant and fragrant tableau. Every few feet along the table, golden lanterns cast a warm, flickering light, accentuating the magical atmosphere.

Ru had also set up a buffet table laden with an array of dishes. There were platters of fresh salads made from locally sourced produce, roasted meats, an assortment of cheeses, freshly baked bread, and, of course, a variety of desserts.

As guests arrived, their expressions transformed from polite curiosity to genuine awe. Many couldn't believe the transformation of the garden and the level of detail that Ru had poured into this gathering.

Mr H, wrapped in a shawl with floral patterns that mirrored the garden's blooms, whispered to Ru,

"This is breathtaking, dear. It feels like we've stepped into a Midsummer Night's Dream."

Ru looked around the table and felt tangible joy and love for each person who was there. Just as dessert was served, Mr Smithson pulled her to the side. They gazed up at the oak tree and he pulled out an envelope from his inside pocket.

"I loved Lynn so very much. She was a pillar of this community and always a safe pair of hands. Especially me. I heard about your plans for her memorial garden initiative and I wanted to give you something. It wouldn't be like anything you were on during your time in London, but hopefully it would be enough to keep you going alongside your work at Shipman's."

Ru took the envelope and opened it. Her eyes widened at the number written in the small box on the cheque. She looked up at Mr Smithson, her eyes filled with tears of gratitude and surprise.

"I... I don't even know what to say," she murmured, holding the cheque in her trembling hand. Mr Smithson placed a reassuring hand on her shoulder.

"You don't need to say anything."

Ru hugged the elderly man, her heart filled with emotion.

"Thank you. This is beyond generous. It's not just the amount, it's the sentiment behind it."

He smiled warmly at her, his eyes twinkling.

"Lynn always spoke so highly of you, and she'd be so proud to see all you're doing. This garden initiative is a beautiful way to remember her, and I'm just glad I could be a part of it."

As they rejoined the table, the evening, already filled with joy and gratitude, became even more special with Mr Smithson's generous gesture. The pastel skies turned into deep shades of blue as conversations bubbled and laughter filled the air.

Each person represented someone special who had shaped her welcoming into the community. At the head of the table was Mrs H, her floral shawl now draped across her lap. She had been the first friendly face and a beacon of wisdom. Her nurturing spirit had eased Ru's transition, and the memory of their first shared pot of tea still warmed Ru's heart.

Beside her was Milly and Beth who had taught Ru the meaning of friendship. They're walking group provided joy and clarity when they all needed it most.

Daniel, of course, held a special place. He was more than just a helper in the garden. He was the one who had made her heart race, who had shared deep conversations under starry skies and had become an integral part of her life in Puckleworth.

Sophie Lang, the astute real estate agent, sat animatedly discussing a new property. Ru respected her for her business acumen and appreciated the genuine care with which she handled her clients. Their professional relationship was morphing into a bond over shared community interests.

Across from Sophie was Mr Smithson. His generous gesture tonight spoke volumes, but it wasn't just about the cheque. It was his stories of Auntie Lynn, their shared memories, and the love he had for the community that resonated deeply with Ru.

Interspersed were others - members from the Friends Committee, Sally and Duncan who had warmly welcomed into their workforce, and even the local postman, who always had a kind word and a wave.

Ru took a moment to absorb the scene before her. The lanterns cast a gentle glow, reflecting in the eyes of her friends. The music, soft and melodic, created a background to the symphony of laughter and conversations. She raised her glass, capturing everyone's attention.

"To new beginnings, to cherished memories, and to a community that has welcomed me with open arms," she toasted. There was a chorus of agreement, glasses clinking together. The night, brimming with love and camaraderie, showed that home wasn't just a place, but a feeling, woven together by the people who filled one's life.

Chapter Thirty

The day of completion had arrived. Ru sat at the kitchen table, her knees bouncing with nerves and excitement. The kettle whistled in the background, and Moss, always attuned to Ru's moods, brushed against her leg, offering silent comfort. Ru's mind raced with thoughts and plans for the land, every idea fuelled by her vision and passion for community building. Yet, amidst the excitement, the weight of responsibility loomed large. Her phone buzzed, startling her from her thoughts. An incoming call from Sophie flashed on the screen.

"Hello?"

"Ru," Sophie's familiar voice came through, bright and cheerful, "It's official! Congratulations! The plot is now yours."

A rush of emotions overwhelmed her. Elation, relief, gratitude and a touch of anxiety all jumbled together. "Thank you, Sophie. Truly. This wouldn't have been possible without your guidance."

"Well, all I did was facilitate. Your vision and determination did the rest. Puckleworth is in for something special. I can feel it."

The two chatted for a few more minutes, discussing the next steps, before hanging up. Ru sat back, allowing the reality to sink in. Her dream was no longer just a dream; it was a tangible reality. A blank canvas awaiting her touch, her ideas and her heart.

Moss jumped onto the table, nudging her hand with his head. Ru chuckled, petting him.

"We did it, Moss. Now, let's create something beautiful."

She texted Daniel to meet her at the plot, put on her aunt's gardening overalls and headed down straight away. As she turned the corner, Daniel was already there. He leant against a fence post, he stood with a picnic blanket in one hand and a bottle of champagne in the other.

The plot was serene, with birdsong filling the air and a gentle breeze rustling the grass. The land stretched out before them, an unmarked slate, holding endless potential. They both sat down, the blanket soft beneath them, the world suddenly narrowing down to just the two of them in this vast space.

Daniel popped open the champagne, the bubbly liquid foaming and filling the glasses he'd thoughtfully brought along.

"To new beginnings and dreams turned into reality," he toasted, his eyes locked onto hers. Ru clinked her glass against his, her eyes shining with emotion.

"To us, and the adventures ahead."

They sipped their champagne, letting the moment sink in. The weight of the purchase, the commitment and her dreams for the space wrapped around them. There was also a sense of joy, of possibility, and of love.

After a while, Ru pulled out a notebook and began sharing her immediate plans with Daniel. They spoke animatedly, their fingers tracing imagined paths and spots on the ground, envisioning flower beds, community areas and small market stalls. Daniel, ever the practical one, jotted down notes and offered insights on landscaping and structural logistics.

The bottle of champagne slowly emptied, their laughter echoed, and their fingers entwined. As the first stars appeared, Daniel leaned over, capturing Ru's lips with his own. In that kiss, everything rushed back. The promise of tomorrow, the joy of the present, and the reverence for the journey.

Chapter Thirty One

The support from the Puckleworth community was overwhelming. Word spread quickly, and it wasn't just monetary donations that came in. Many offered their time, skills and resources. From landscape designers volunteering their expertise to local farmers providing young saplings and seeds, the project had quickly evolved into a true community endeavour.

A letter was delivered to Ru's doorstep. It was from Lillian, the elderly woman who ran the small bookstore in town. She proposed setting up a small corner inside the memorial garden, a place where people could read about plants, nature and sustainability. Alongside her proposal, she donated several books to kick start the garden's library.

Beth suggested classes during the school holidays for children, teaching them the basics of planting, the importance of each season, and the joys of harvesting. The idea was to instil a love for nature and teach them the value of hard work and patience.

Daniel took the lead on many fronts. He coordinated with local suppliers for soil, compost and tools. He also rallied the youth, setting up weekend workshops to prepare the land.

One evening, after a long day of work, the community gathered at the plot for a potluck dinner to celebrate the opening of the gardens. As Ru looked around, she saw the faces of Puckleworth's residents lit up by the soft glow of lanterns.

Children played around, their laughter echoing, while the adults shared stories, dishes, and dreams for the garden.

Ru, her eyes glistening with unshed tears as she looked over to the entrance. There stood clutching a bouquet was her mum. She looked radiant, her complexion a warmer and healthier since the last time she'd seen her.

For a moment, the world seemed to stop. All the memories, the pain, the distance and the complicated history between them hovered in the space between the mother and daughter.

Ru's heart raced, a flurry of emotions surging within her. She hadn't expected her mum to be here, especially not on this significant day. The tension in the air was palpable as they locked eyes. Both searching for the right words, the right way to bridge the distance that had grown between them over the years.

Taking a deep breath, Ru's mum took a tentative step forward, her voice soft and trembling.

"Ruth... I... I just wanted to see you. To see this place you've been writing about in your letters. I received them all. I'm sorry I didn't write back. Every time I tried the words wouldn't come out."

Ru stood still, her emotions a whirlwind. But as she took in her mother's appearance, the visible changes, the vulnerability in her eyes, something shifted inside her.

"Mum." Her voice choked with emotion.

The bouquet dropped to the ground as the two women rushed towards each other, the past momentarily forgotten in the fierce embrace they shared. They clung to each other, tears flowing freely, letting out years of pent-up emotions, regrets, and unsaid words.

After what felt like an eternity, they pulled apart, both wiping their eyes. Ru's mum took a deep breath.

"I'm sorry. I know I've made mistakes, so many mistakes. But seeing you now, the life you've built, fills me with so much pride."

Ru nodded, trying to find her voice amidst the emotions.

"It's been hard, but I've found a place where I belong. And I've missed you."

Her mum reached out, tucking a stray hair behind Ru's ear.

"I've missed you too, love."

Daniel, who had been watching from a distance, approached with understanding in his eyes. Ru introduced him, and as the three of them stood there, a new chapter unfolded.

The presence of Ru's mum brought up old wounds, but it also offered an opportunity for healing and understanding. The plot of land, which symbolises new beginnings for Ru, now became a beacon of hope for her relationship with her mother.

Weeks turned into months, and with collective effort, the barren plot transformed. Raised beds lined with vegetables and herbs, fruit trees casting their young shadows, and a small gazebo in the centre.

A plaque sat on the entwine branched archway entrance, reading: *"Auntie Lynn's Memorial Garden: A testament to love, legacy, and community."*

Every time residents of Puckleworth walked under that archway, there was a palpable sense of pride. Not just in the blooming flora or the carefully constructed spaces within, but in what the garden represented.

Local children often gathered around the plot, learning about the plants from volunteers, many of whom had learned their gardening skills from Auntie Lynn herself. Laughter and giggles echoed as they chased butterflies or hunted for the ripest tomatoes. Elderly community members would often be seen resting under the shade of the gazebo, reminiscing about old times or knitting together, their fingers working deftly even as they shared stories with younger generations.

Ru often hosted workshops, teaching interested individuals about sustainable gardening, organic practices and the importance of local produce. With her experience in floristry, she also held sessions on flower arrangements, weaving in tales of her aunt and the deep connection she felt with every petal and leaf.

Every fortnight, a small farmers' market would spring up, allowing locals to sell their produce and crafts. The initiative not only boosted the local economy but also fostered a sense of camaraderie amongst the residents.

One particularly touching addition to the garden was a small corner dedicated to storytelling. Mrs H took it upon herself to regale young listeners with tales from Puckleworth's history, often including the many adventures she had experienced with Auntie Lynn. The garden wasn't just her legacy; it was a living entity that was continually growing, changing, and adapting, much like the community it served.

As Ru sat on a bench one evening, watching the sun cast its golden hue over the garden, she felt a deep sense of fulfilment. The garden was her dream realised, but it was also so much more. It was Auntie Lynn's memory immortalised, a community's spirit solidified, and the fact that with love, dedication and unity, any dream, no matter how big, could become a reality.

Printed in Great Britain
by Amazon